the Jewels

of Sutton Avenue

the Jewels

of Sutton Avenue

Barbara Lewis

TATE PUBLISHING & *Enterprises*

The Jewels of Sutton Avenue
Copyright © 2011 by Barbara Lewis. All rights reserved.

This novel is a work of fiction. Names, descriptions, entities, and incidents included in the story are products of the author's imagination. Any resemblance to actual persons, events, and entities is entirely coincidental.

The opinions expressed by the author are not necessarily those of Tate Publishing, LLC.

Published by Tate Publishing & Enterprises, LLC
127 E. Trade Center Terrace | Mustang, Oklahoma 73064 USA
1.888.361.9473 | www.tatepublishing.com

Tate Publishing is committed to excellence in the publishing industry. The company reflects the philosophy established by the founders, based on Psalm 68:11,
"The Lord gave the word and great was the company of those who published it."

Book design copyright © 2011 by Tate Publishing, LLC. All rights reserved.
Cover design by Rebekah Garibay
Interior design by Sarah Kirchen

Published in the United States of America

ISBN: 978-1-61777-173-6
1. Fiction / Family Life
2. Fiction / Contemporary Women
11.02.16

For my parents; my father who supported me
and my beloved mother, who nurtured my
creativity and allowed me the time and space
to dream. Her children were her jewels.

Marie McFarland, my library teacher at Copernicus
Grammar School; gone but not forgotten. She
taught me the love of reading and instilled in
me pride and confidence in my talent.

TABLE OF CONTENTS

FOREWORD

When Barbara asked me to write the foreword for her book, I recalled the years of work she's put into her craft. She's been an actress, producer, director, and playwright. She's created her own theater company, "Faye's Keylight Theatre Company" for her original productions. Yet she always worked full time at another job. Compelled to write a novel, she gave full attention to her muse. The result is *The Jewels of Sutton Avenue*, a stirring novel about a family's love for each other. Beautifully written with compassion and clarity, the reader is introduced to questions of sacrifice and family responsibility.

The Jewels of Sutton Avenue is based on her third original stage play, *Jewels*. I first met Barbara in the early 1990s, shortly after she had written her first play, *Only Sixteen*, an extremely moving drama about teenage pregnancy. When I saw it performed by her production company, there were few dry eyes in the house thanks to her sensitive direction. I have been amazed by Barbara's creativity and stamina all these years. I look forward to more of her work and would love to see *The Jewels of Sutton Avenue* on the big screen. I hope you enjoy reading this book as much as I did. It gives voice to the strength and value of our families and would be a welcome addition to any school's reading curriculum.

—Carol Kurz, September 19, 2010

I have known Barbara Anne Lewis for the past twenty years as we worked together in a setting to promote the recovery and strengths of children and adolescents with emotional and developmental difficulties. The time I first met her, she was inspiring everyone at the center, as she put on one of her first plays in the basement of the center, using the children as actors and actresses. It is rare in life when you meet someone with such amazing talent for storytelling and writing and insight into the emotional world of her characters. Over the years, I know that as a playwright and director she has sacrificed and poured her heart and soul into her work, as she was so dedicated and passionate about the arts and determined to have the voices of these characters heard by a broader audience, first in Chicago, then other parts of the country. Barbara is a powerful woman who never gave up on her dream in spite of major setbacks and challenges, and I am so excited that she is about to share her "people magic" with the world. Consider yourself fortunate as you are about to read a jewel of a book written by one of America's newest and hottest authors.

—Alexis Lybrook Taubert, Ph.D.
Clinical Psychologist/Friend

REFLECTION

The members of the Morgan family were respected residents in their Detroit neighborhood. They lived on a picturesque street of neat bungalows with manicured lawns. The Morgan house was the third one from the corner—3206 Sutton Avenue, a two-story brick. Seven concrete steps led to the wraparound front porch, which housed a swing. The swing was the house's biggest selling point. In the days before air conditioning, families spent hot summer nights on the front porch. The massive front door with a built-in mail slot opened to the foyer.

The Morgan house was the only one on the street with a side driveway and a two-car garage. The block had large trees; most people had gardens in their backyards. The huge weeping willow trees on Sutton Avenue sloped over the front lawns, providing shade and blocking the hot sun in summer. The trees branches were heavy with snow and icicles in winter like a Christmas painting; in autumn they were beautiful with multi-colored leaves; in spring for a short time they were filled with rose-tinted blossoms.

Shelton and Mae Morgan lived in this house with their four daughters. Shelton Curtis Morgan was born in Eagle Mill, Arkansas. One of four children, he was the youngest son born to Mary and Rodell. Eagle Mill was famous for its grinding poverty. As in all pre-integration rural southern towns, it was governed by the white citizenship. To escape his hand-to-mouth existence, Shelton left home at fifteen to join his oldest sister Helen and her husband in Detroit. They lived in a tiny three-room walkup. Shelton slept on the couch in the living room. Helen was a waitress in a diner, and she eventually got him a dishwashing job. He worked there three months. The fourth month he lied about his age and got a job at the Ford Motor Company.

When he first saw Mae Hudson, he thought she was an angel come down to visit from heaven. Their courtship was short but intense. Six months from the day he first met her, he asked her to be his wife. Shelton married Mae when he was twenty-one. She was eighteen and in the full glow of her youthful beauty. She was five feet four inches to his six feet and had to get up on tiptoes to kiss him when the minister pronounced them man and wife. Mae's upbringing had been the exact opposite of her husband's; she was born and raised in Atlanta, Georgia. Her father was a store keeper, and her mother stayed home and pampered her five daughters. They quickly had three children two years apart, all girls. Mae loved her girls, and she always thought of herself as a girls' mother. She gave her daughters gemstone names: Pearl, Diamond, and Topaz.

When Pearl was eighteen, Diamond sixteen, and Topaz fourteen, Mae and Shelton were shocked to find out they were expecting another baby. They did not find out until she was five months pregnant and at age thirty-eight. She was afraid her body couldn't bear another pregnancy. After they prayed together, she was satisfied it was God's will, and his grace would see her through the pregnancy. Ruby, their fourth girl, was born completely healthy and completed the gemstone theme.

When Ruby was three months old, Shelton insisted they must have a professional family picture. The pride he felt was captured on film. Pearl was a lovely young woman, very much like Mae in character, but physically she was all Morgan. She looked like his mother with her full lips and regal carriage. Diamond, considered by all to be the most glamorous sister, looked like a movie star with her long auburn hair flowing around her shoulders. Topaz's sweetness showed through the celluloid, along with her high cheekbones and ruddy complexion. Ruby was so pretty she could only be described as a real baby doll. He hung the picture in the foyer so that it was the last thing he saw before leaving in the morning and the first thing he saw when he came home. It was more than a house; it was a sanctuary. It was one of the standouts of the block before the fire. Now it was a vacant lot overgrown with weeds and debris.

Two women moved arm in arm through the abandoned lot. One was middle aged, and she moved slowly and cautiously to protect swollen ankles developed from years of walking and standing on concrete floors. The other was younger with quick steps and the graceful, fluid moves of a dancer. In the area that used to be the back porch, two steps remained, and they sat down.

Topaz sighed. "The best seats in the house. I used to come out and sit on this porch for hours and look at the stars. Remember the peach tree? I can still smell the peaches. Mama would make the best peach jelly."

Ruby frowned. "That's just your imagination, Topaz. I don't smell anything but old wood. You're just feeling sentimental because it's our first time back since that night."

Topaz's eyes scanned the lot and were moist with silent tears. Her voice was filled with emotion as she spoke. "I'm glad Daddy's not here to see this. He worked so hard to get us out of the projects."

"I know the story. Pearl told me every day."

"Ruby, why do you always reject your past?"

"Because it's the past the way you Diamond, and Pearl see it. I always felt separate and apart from the three of you. You all grew up together. I was the baby. Even Mama and Daddy are distant memories to me."

"I hate to hear you talk like that. How can you say that? Ruby girl, Pearl devoted her life to you."

"I know. She could have been a minister's wife. She quit school. You'll never understand how guilty that makes me feel. I know you all think the fire is the worst thing that could have happened to us, but I don't regret it. It set us all free, especially Pearl."

"No, Ruby, the fire was bad, but it was far from the worst thing we had to face. Nothing compares to that black Tuesday. The day our lives changed forever..."

The day their lives changed forever, Pearl was a senior in college attending Wayne State in math class. In four short months, she and Diamond would graduate and become the first college graduates in the Morgan family. She was marking the days off on the calendar. Because she hated math, she had put this class off until she was told that she had to have this credit to graduate. Diamond was her tutor, and with her help, she was able to maintain at least a C average. One Tuesday morning, a day that started like any other day, she was daydreaming in class when Professor Gill called her to the desk and told her to report to the office. There was a message from home. She was apprehensive as she walked down the hall. Why would she have a message from home? What could be happening? When she left for school that morning, nobody was sick. She looked at the hall clock on the way to the office. It was a little after two p.m.; her father was still at work. Her mother would probably be cooking dinner, and Diamond and Topaz were in school. Little Ruby was in her first semester in kindergarten, and her mother would be picking her up at three p.m. On the way to the office she ran into Leon Finny, the smoothest boy in school. He was always flirting with her, and she liked it.

Leon glided up to her. "Miss Pearl, beauty from the sea, you are the luckiest girl in Wayne State."

Pearl, trying not to blush, said, "Leon Finney, are you crazy?"

Leon, not put off, said, "I'm a little bit crazy about you, Pearl, and the only thing that could make graduation day and night complete is you being my date."

"Day and night?"

With a smile, Leon said, "Yes, ma'am, for the banquet after graduation and the dance that night. Say yes, and that will seal the deal."

Being coy as Diamond had taught her, she said, "I'll think about it."

He teased her and said, "Don't think too long. You might think wrong." She giggled, and he winked as he walked away. She temporarily got lost in this and lingered for a second before remembering she was on her way to the office.

When she got to the office, she knew right away that something was wrong. The dean pulled out a chair for her and held her hand as he began to speak. Dean Combs was a comforting man with receding gray hair. His eyes were warm and kind. He spoke in measured tones.

"Ms. Morgan, I regret that I have some sad news to tell you. I received a call from the hospital. There has been a tragic accident." Pearl steadied herself in the chair, preparing for the worst. She was barely able to speak.

"What kind of accident?"

As Dean Combs continued his words were slower and slower. "A car accident." He reached and held both her hands now. "Your mother and father were thrown from their car and died instantly. I am so terribly sorry."

His words were like cymbals in her head. She instantly covered her ears to try to silence his words. Pearl began to unravel like a ball of twine. She felt like she was drowning in a pool of water and could not get her breath. The room was spinning around her, and she could not find her center. The dean's words became a blur. She was sure that he was still talking. She saw his lips moving, but she could no longer hear anything.

A million images were racing through her head. All she could see were her father and mother's faces. All she could hear was their voices.

Pearl, shaken, asked, "Please, Dean, could I have a sip of water? My mouth is so dry. It feels like it's full of cotton."

"Of course you can, I'll be right back. He scurried down the hall and quickly returned with a paper cup of water. "Here you are." The water began to run down Pearl's chin, and he took the cup from her. "Let me help you with this. Drink slowly. Do you want some more?"

"No this is enough. How did you find out about Mama and Daddy?"

"Just about thirty minutes ago, the hospital called."

"Why did they call here?"

"It seems your father had your name and Wayne State as an emergency contact in his wallet. The admitting doctor told me he and your mother were hit by an oncoming car that ran the stop light and never stopped. It was a hit and run."

"My sisters don't know yet? I have to tell them."

"No, dear, to the best of my knowledge this is the only call the hospital made."

"Let me tell my secretary that I will be leaving for the day. Then I will drive you home."

"No that's not necessary. I would rather walk. It's not that far."

"Nonsense, you don't need to be alone right now. It's not up for debate, Miss Morgan. I consider this my obligation."

"Dean Combs, I do need to walk very much. I need air in my lungs, plus I have so much to think about, and I can only do that alone." Sensing the desperation in her tone, Dean Combs decided this was not the time to push.

"Miss Morgan, please be careful, and promise me you'll call if there's anything I can do for you and your family."

"I promise."

Strangely, Pearl did not cry. She felt like she had stepped outside her body and was looking in. Dean Combs left so that she could be alone and told her to stay in the room as long as she needed. Pearl could not move. She looked out of the window and saw students and faculty moving about the campus talking and laughing, and she was instantly angry with them. *How could they act as though nothing had happened? What gave them the right to be happy?* Her whole world was different and would never be the same again. She was afraid to leave the room because she knew this was her last chance to be weak. From this day on she would have to somehow summon the strength to take care of her sisters and keep their lives as normal as possible.

When she got home, Diamond was on the front porch. She was concerned because her mother was not home. She had called the church, and she wasn't there.

"Where could she be? Where's Topaz?" Pearl sat on the step next to Diamond and began to speak. "I got some bad news today at school."

"What happened? You failed a math test?"

"It was about Mama and Daddy."

"Why would you hear anything about them at school?"

"Diamond, Mama and Daddy were in a car accident today."

"Who told you this?"

"Dean Combs called me out of class today. Ford Hospital called the school. We have to go see them, Diamond."

"What? Pearl, are they hurt bad?"

"I wish they were." For the first time since she sat on the porch, Pearl buried her head in her hands. "They're gone. Diamond, Mama and Daddy died today. It was a hit and—" But before she could finish the story, Diamond had jumped off the porch and was running down the block crying. Pearl ran after her and held her in her arms. Diamond was crying as though her heart would break. Her questions were coming in rapid speed between her sobs.

"Why Mama and Daddy? They never did anything to anybody. Why would God let this happen to them? I'll never go to church again." Pearl did not say a word. She had no answers for these questions. Diamond was just saying out loud the thoughts that were in her heart.

Topaz was in the office of Carver Elementary to inform the school clerk that she was picking up her little sister, Ruby, for her mother. Mrs. Winston introduced herself.

"I don't believe we've met. I'm Mrs. Winston, the school clerk, and you are?"

"Topaz Morgan. Ruby's sister. I came to pick her up for my mother."

"Of course you can take your little sister home, but I'm surprised your mother isn't here. You can set a watch by Mrs. Morgan. She's here every day, three fifteen on the dot. I hope she's not sick."

"No, something important must have come up. She'll tell you about it tomorrow." When Ruby was brought to the office and saw Topaz, she began to pout.

"Where is Mama?"

"She's not here. I came to take you home today." Ruby turned her back and refused to talk.

"You can see Mama when you get home. If you talk to me we can go by Miss Arnold's Store on the way home and get—let's see—maybe some candy."

"For real? Can we get peppermint sticks, red and green?"

"Only if it's a secret just between you and me. Nobody else can know."

"Nobody?"

"Not Pearl or Diamond or Mama. Especially Mama. You know how she hates junk food before dinner." Ruby smiled and hugged her.

Off they went to Arnold's candy store, where her mother kept an account for the girls so that they could get treats.

As usual everyone in the store was enchanted with Ruby. She was so cute; she had such a pretty smile. Ruby loved the attention. Ms. Arnold gave her three peppermint sticks and told Topaz it was on the house. "A little girl this pretty should have whatever she wants."

Pearl and Diamond were in the house when Topaz and Ruby came in laughing. Ruby was calling, "Mama, Mama! I made a kite today at school all by myself." Pearl grabbed her and hugged her. "Let me see this pretty kite you made all by yourself."

Ruby proudly announced, "Miss Cater helped me just a little bit. The colors are so bright. Green is my favorite color. Where is Mama?"

Pearl avoided the question. "Saturday morning I'm going to take you and this pretty green kite all the way over to Belle Isle Park, and we'll fly it all afternoon."

Diamond was sitting at the kitchen table, and Topaz knew immediately that something was wrong. Her eyes were red-rimmed, and she looked vacant.

Probably a breakup with a boy, Topaz thought. Diamond was so dramatic when it came to matters of the heart.

She avoided Diamond and asked Pearl, "Where is Mama?"

Pearl was about to answer, but she wanted to protect Ruby. "Ruby, go upstairs, and take your school shoes off. And don't forget to hang up your sweater."

Ruby whined, "Do I have to do it right now?"

"Yes, right now."

Topaz chimed in, "Do what Pearl says. You know when Mama is not home Pearl is in charge."

Ruby turned to go upstairs, mumbling on the way, "I'll be glad when Mama gets home."

"Topaz, sit down."

"What's going on?"

Pearl again repeated the story. Each time she said the words, her heart ached a little more. Topaz's body was rigid, and she quietly cried, tears streaming down her cheeks. When she was finally able to find her voice, it was a childlike frightened plea.

"What's going to happen to us? What are we going to do without Mama and Daddy? Who's going to take care of Ruby?"

Before Pearl could answer, the telephone rang. She went to the living room to answer it, and Topaz and Diamond sat facing each other in silence. When Pearl returned, Topaz asked, "Who's going to take care of Ruby?"

Pearl answered her, "We have to think about that later. That was the hospital, spelling out the words for Ruby's sake. They want someone to come in and take care of the paperwork, so Mama and Daddy can be released to..." Her words were whispers now. Topaz had to almost read her lips to understand what she was saying.

"Call Bishop King, and ask him to meet us at the hospital. Mama and Daddy would want him to be there." Diamond protested and said she did not want to go to the hospital. Pearl held her hand and looked straight into her eyes. "We are the oldest, and we have to go. Topaz has to stay here with Ruby."

Fear jumped into Topaz's eyes, "I can't tell Ruby." She and Diamond both looked at Pearl.

"I will tell her when we get back. Make sure she eats dinner. Make pancakes for her. She loves pancakes."

"For dinner?" Topaz asked.

Pearl told Topaz, "She is five years old and an orphan. Let's try to give her what she wants." Topaz began to slowly climb the stairs to attend to Ruby. Her legs were so heavy she felt like she was walking in quicksand.

Pearl and Diamond walked hand-in-hand out the front door. They went to the corner to the bus stop to wait for the number eleven bus—the only one that went straight to the hospital. When the bus came, they stepped on. Pearl paid their fares, and they moved to seats in the back and sat like zombies the entire ride. After approximately twenty minutes, the bus was pulling into Henry Ford Hospital. The moment they dreaded was approaching fast. This was the proof that this awful day was indeed a reality. It was not just a nightmare or a mistake. This was really happening. They held each other tightly as if they were both supporting each other. When they entered the hospital, Pearl looked at the clock—four forty-five p.m. Living proof that this nightmare was true. She really had lost her mother and father.

The first face they saw in the lobby was Bishop King's. Bishop King was a short, stocky man with coal black hair and matching skin tone. His body was shaped like a big teddy bear. He and Sister King had been married for ten years but were childless. Every Sunday in testifying service, Sister King would ask for prayer for God to bless her womb. He walked over and hugged them both.

"When I got your call, I came right away. I was at the supper table, but I just pushed my food to the side, put my shoes on, and walked out of the door. I even waited until I got here to call Sister King to tell her where I am. This is a black day; Shelton and Mae were two of God's angels. I just got through talking to the doctors; they told me that it happened instantly, so thank the Master they didn't have to suffer. If you want me to, I will take care of the identification and fill out any papers the hospital needs. You girls have been through enough today. Your father had good insurance at Ford. One thing you girls won't have to worry about is money. Shelton was a good man. He provided for his family. I remember just last month he was talking about how he made Pearl the beneficiary because she was going to be a college graduate and she would be smart and fair enough to handle the money. I wonder if God was trying to tell him something. Just last month. The LORD moves in mysterious ways, mysterious ways."

Diamond thanked him right away. Pearl was reluctant to hand over this duty, but she didn't have the will to contest it, so she nodded yes also. She and Diamond stumbled into the couches in the lobby and sat together holding hands in silence.

Bishop King returned and told them that the bodies were going to be moved to Crane's Funeral Home, and they could all talk about the service arrangements tomorrow.

"I asked Sister King to go pick up Ruby, so you girls don't have to worry about taking care of her these next difficult days."

Pearl answered quickly, "No! I have to explain to her what happened today. She doesn't even know yet. She needs to stay at home with us."

Bishop King frowned. "Sister King can certainly tell Ruby, and we want to be of service and take as many burdens from your shoulders as possible. From this day on, you girls are going to need help with Ruby. Both Sister King and I considered Mae and Shelton family, and I know they would want us to look out for y'all."

Pearl knew deep inside her soul that her parents would not want them to be separated and that she must make sure that the family stayed together.

"Bishop King, you know how much we love you and Sister King, and we appreciate so much you coming here. But after tonight, Ruby needs to come home and be with us, her family. We have to be her mother and father now. Mama and Daddy would want us to stay together now."

Bishop King was visibly shaken. "Of course, Pearl, if that is what you want, that's what it will be."

Sister King brought Ruby home the next morning, and she ran to Pearl crying. Against Pearl's better wishes, Sister King had told Ruby about her parents, and she was inconsolable.

Pearl cradled her in her lap, "Come on, baby. Stop crying. Wipe your eyes. There's no need to cry. Do you know how lucky you are? You have two angels watching over you."

"Where?

"In heaven. That's where Mama and Daddy went. They're angels now. God knew they were special, and he wanted them to live with him. They still love us, and all your life they will watch over you and protect you."

This stilled her sobs, and she rested in Pearl's lap.

Sister King apologized. "I'm sorry if I overstepped. I just thought the child should know. She kept asking for her mama, and I didn't want to lie to her."

"There's some hot coffee on the stove, and Sister Clay dropped off some coffee cake this morning fresh from the bakery. Let me get you some."

"No, baby, food is the last thing on my mind this morning. Mae's spirit is everywhere in this house, especially in the kitchen. I can see and feel Mae all around me. Just about now she would be making her good biscuits, flour on her hands and apron, and we would be talking about something that happened in church Sunday. LORD, this kitchen is empty without Mae Morgan."

Topaz was coming down the stairs and heard her and collapsed in tears. Ruby ran to Topaz and began to cry again. Pearl gently led Sister King to the front door. When Sister King was in her car and out of sight, Pearl sat on the front porch and finally broke down and cried and prayed.

"Mama, Daddy, LORD, please give me the wisdom to know what to do. I'm so scared. What is going to happen to us?"

TRANSITION

On the day of the funeral, it was an unusually warm spring morning. It was the season of lilacs, daisies, young green grass, ice-blue skies, sudden storms, and lazy afternoons. Spring was the season of beginnings, and now forever for the Morgan sisters, the season of endings. The sun was shining brightly through the bedroom window; the rays were so bright that Diamond got up and closed the curtains. She looked over at Topaz in her twin bed, but she was sound asleep. She couldn't be that sleepy; she was probably afraid to wake up and face the day.

The house was completely still, no noise going on anywhere. Diamond moved around the house, her mind drifting back to last week. Just seven days ago things were so different. Usually Ruby was up and running around the house by now. Mama would be cooking breakfast; and the girls could smell the bacon and coffee scents floating up the staircase. Daddy would be gone when they got up, and Mama would have already packed his lunch from dinner leftovers. Pearl rode with Daddy in the morning. Wayne State was three blocks from his job, and he and Pearl treasured their private time together. Mama had to force them to eat oatmeal. They all hated oatmeal and protested every morning, but Mama insisted it was good for them and they should just eat it, swearing, "One day you will all thank me." Diamond spoke out loud to herself, "If I could have Mama just one more hour, I would eat all the oatmeal in the world."

It was seven thirty a.m. Since all of them had been out of school that week, their whole schedule was off. One hour would bleed into the next, and before they knew it, the day was over. Pearl kept herself busy distracting Ruby; she played Candyland with her over and over again, taught her how to stay in the lines in her coloring book, and flew the kite that Mama never got to see.

When Pearl heard Ruby laughing, she wondered if she really understood what had happened to Mama and Daddy. The radio had not been on all week. Everybody was trying to keep the world outside and pretend that life was inside those walls. Conversation was nonexistent. They only talked to each other when it was absolutely necessary. Pearl and Topaz went to bed every night at eight p.m.

The church ladies and especially Sister King were in and out every day, bringing food and fresh laundry. The refrigerator was full of food, but nobody was eating it. The tin foil became shrouds for the contents of the dishes.

Topaz was starting to move restlessly in the bed. "What time is it?" she asked.

"It's almost eight a.m."

"It's still early. We don't have to be at the church until noon, and we still have time to sleep." Topaz turned over and put the pillow over her head. Diamond took the pillow away. "We do need to get up. We have to bathe, and we all need time get in the bathroom. The car will be here at eleven, and we don't want to make them wait for us." Topaz looked at her through heavy-lidded eyes.

"Who's fixing breakfast? I don't hear anybody downstairs. I'm not hungry, but I just think somebody should fix breakfast. Where's Pearl?"

"I don't know. The only reason I haven't gone to her room is because I don't want to wake up Ruby. She's been sleeping with Pearl all week." Topaz was sitting on the edge of the bed now.

Topaz pinned up Diamond's hair so that she could take a bath and start to make the beds in the room just as she had done every other ordinary day. When she was fluffing her pillow, she looked up and saw Pearl in the doorway.

"How long have you been standing there?"

"Not long. I just wanted to see if you and Diamond were up. We need to get organized. Remember we want to make Daddy and Mama proud of us today." Her eyes were moist. It was the first time Topaz had seen this, and she immediately walked over and hugged her. After a few moments, Pearl gently pulled away and changed the subject. She spoke without looking at Topaz, afraid to meet her eyes.

"I'm going to dress Ruby in all white today. The dress she got for Easter will be perfect. I bathed her last night, and I took my bath very early this morning. You and Diamond have the bathroom all to yourselves. I'm going downstairs to call the florist to see if the flowers are at the church and make breakfast for Ruby. As soon as Diamond comes out of the bathroom, it's your turn. Tell Diamond not so much lipstick today, please!"

Diamond came out of the bedroom all clean and scrubbed. The steam from the bathroom gave her a rosy glow.

"Pearl said don't put on too much lipstick today."

"Why?"

"I guess she wants us to look plain. I don't know. She just said it."

"I don't care what Pearl said. Lipstick is my favorite thing. I can't go out the front door without my lipstick."

Topaz went into the bathroom, and Diamond went back to the room to pick out her outfit. She chose a two-piece navy blue suit with white cuffs and collar. The jacket had a fitted waist, and the skirt was a full circle. Mama always loved her in this suit; she said it was so ladylike, and she wanted to please her today. In her hair ornament drawer she picked out a rhinestone barrette but decided against it because Pearl would probably say it was too flashy. Instead she chose a plain white headband. Today she didn't wear lipstick. When she finished dressing, she went downstairs to sit on the living room couch to wait for everybody else. She wanted this time alone to just sit and look out the window.

Topaz came from the bathroom smelling like baby powder. She loved the clean fresh smell of baby products. They were her only cosmetics: baby oil, baby soap, baby lotion, and baby powder. The dresser in her and Diamond's room looked almost schizophrenic. Topaz's side was covered with baby products, and Diamond's side was loaded with perfume bottles and makeup—one woman avoiding adulthood and another one rushing to meet it.

Topaz was unsure of what to wear, and they didn't talk about the service or clothes that week. She went to the church clothes side of the closet and closed her eyes; she decided that wherever her hand rested was the outfit she was going to wear. When she opened her eyes, she was touching her plaid jumper with the real silk orange blouse that was her birthday present last year.

"I need to rethink this. Plaid is not good for a funeral service, and maybe the orange is too bright." Every time she tried to be spontaneous she couldn't pull it off. She finally chose old faithful—a black skirt and her white ruffled blouse. She couldn't go wrong with black and white to make the outfit a little dressier; she wore Diamond's black and white spectator pumps. She didn't even look at herself in the mirror. This was one day she didn't care how she looked. When she passed Pearl's room, she was braiding white ribbon into Ruby's hair and singing to her. Ruby was dressed all in white, from her head to her toes. She really did look like an angel on top of a Christmas tree. Watching Pearl comb Ruby's hair, Topaz was aware that Pearl looked so much older than she had just last week. She was dressed in her high school graduation suit, pale gray, and today she was wearing Mama's pearls, the ones that Daddy had given her for their twentieth anniversary.

Ruby was singing, "Sunday, Monday, Tuesday, Wednesday, Thursday, Friday, Saturday, and Sunday again. Sunday we go to church."

Pearl patiently told her, "No, honey, today is Saturday, not Sunday."

"Why are we going to church? We go to church on Sunday."

"Remember I told you last night that this is a very special service and a very special day."

"You said we would see Mama and Daddy again. I remember."

At eleven a.m. on the dot, the funeral car pulled up in front of the house. The driver from Crane's Funeral Home walked up the stairs and rang the bell. Diamond was still sitting on the couch, but she could not move. He rang the bell again, and still she was frozen. On the third bell Pearl came running down the steps. She looked at Diamond but did not say a word.

"Good morning, we're ready. There are four of us here, but my little sister can sit on my lap. The next stop about ten blocks away is my uncle James's house. There will be two there, and the last stop just around the corner from the church will be my aunt Inez and her husband so the car will be full. We're coming right out."

Pearl physically pulled Diamond from the couch and led her to the front door. When they pulled up to Uncle James's house, he and Aunt Evelyn were waiting for them on the front porch. Uncle James hugged them;

Aunt Evelyn was frantically dabbing her eyes. The next stop was Aunt Inez's house, and they picked up the rest of the family.

After what seemed to be a lifetime, they were in front of the church. Jones Tabernacle stood majestically in the sun. In that instant Pearl remembered her father saying that he always wanted to go to a church on the corner. They had burned the mortgage on the church last year, and the church had praise service all week. Today the church was overflowing with people. There were so many people that they ran out of obituaries. Bishop King's eulogy was a moving testament to Shelton and Mae's well-lived lives. Pearl lifted Ruby up so that she could say goodbye, and she kissed both her father and mother.

At the cemetery Topaz stayed in the funeral car. She couldn't bring herself to see her parents put in the ground. During the entire service she did not listen to the tributes or sermon; she stared at her father and mother. She did not need anyone to tell her how wonderful they were; she already knew that. What she needed to do was to memorize their faces and burn them into her memory so she would not forget them at this age.

Leaving the cemetery, Sister King pulled Pearl aside. Sister King spoke softly, "You know that me and Bishop King would have no problem keeping Ruby until after you graduate and even longer while you look for a job. You girls have enough on your plates. Mae was like my own sister, and I know in my heart she would expect me to help out now, and I feel I owe her this."

Pearl told her, "I will call you, Sister King, if we need you. The car is waiting to take us back to the church."

The repast was like a banquet. Every inch of every table was covered with food. They had to open all the windows and the side door to get some circulation in the church basement; the people were using up all the oxygen. Pearl and Diamond were going from table to table thanking everyone for coming. Everybody told them over and over again how much they admired their parents. Topaz spent most of the time in the ladies' room. Her stomach was upset. Ruby finally went to sleep in Sister King's arms and slept most of the afternoon. Bishop King took Pearl, Diamond, and Topaz home; Sister King had taken Ruby to her house earlier. Out of the corner of her eye, Pearl saw her tiptoe out, but she was too tired to stop her. Bishop King unloaded the leftover food and tried to stuff it into an already swollen refrigerator. After he left, they all sat in silence until it was time to go to bed. Sunday morning they did not go to church. Everybody overslept, and they were still finding it difficult to get back into the natural rhythm of their lives. Pearl cooked breakfast, and they ate dinner from the leftovers from the church.

Monday morning Diamond and Topaz returned to school. Diamond was due to graduate from college in four months, and she was the valedictorian of her class at Michigan State Teachers College. On April 11 she would be twenty-one and graduate in May. She was required to do her practice teaching for a year, and then she would be a certified teacher. She wanted to be a teacher because it was a profession that would travel well. Anywhere she went she would know that she could always find a job. Pearl was always curious as to where she would want to go; Diamond always shrugged her shoulders.

"Who knows? I might end up in Alaska. Eskimos need to learn to read and write too." Her return to school was awkward for her classmates but not so much for her, because in a strange way she was relieved to have something to do with her days. Schoolwork stopped her from focusing on the tragedy. It was awkward for her classmates and teachers; everybody was scared to talk or laugh around her, and people were constantly hugging her for no reason. Because her teachers and classmates were so uncomfortable, she began to feel sorry for them. By Thursday she decided to bring up the subject herself and take everyone off the hook. She asked permission in every class if she could make a brief statement to tell everyone how much she appreciated and was grateful for their condolences, but she and her family were learning to adjust, and she wanted to be treated as she was before.

Topaz was nineteen and in her freshman year in Wilson Junior College studying nursing. From the time she was a little girl she knew that she wanted to be a nurse. When her mother would take her to the clinic, she always admired Miss Andrews in her sparkling white uniform, and she was always particularly kind to her. On every visit Miss Andrews let her sit at her desk and try on her stiff white hat. When Topaz graduated from high school, she recommended her alma mater and wrote a letter to the dean of admissions on Topaz's behalf. When Topaz returned to school, the students and faculty presented her with a lovely card and a bouquet of violets and roses.

Meanwhile, Sister King was still keeping Ruby. She continued to insist that she was simply helping the family out during their transition. Pearl was annoyed and impatient with the arrangement, but every time she asked the Kings to bring Ruby home, they had another excuse. When Pearl again pressed her about bringing Ruby home, she then insisted in an exasperated tone that she was only keeping Ruby until she finished school. Every time Pearl called and asked to speak to Ruby she was told that she was either in the bathroom or outside playing.

One day on the way to school, Pearl knew instantly what she had to do; she went straight to the dean of studies to withdraw from her classes. The outer office was empty, so she softly knocked on Dean Rogers's partially opened door.

"Ms. Bond is not at her desk. Can I come in?"

"Yes, one of Wayne States' policies is that we are always available to our students. Please come in. Have a seat. How can I help you today?"

"My name is Pearl Morgan, and I'm in the senior class."

"Congratulations, you will be alumnus soon."

"Dean Rogers, I need to talk to you about a personal matter at home. You may or may not know that I recently lost both my parents in a car accident."

"Dean Combs shared your tragedy with me. I'm so sorry."

"That is the reason I'm here today. Things have changed so drastically at home. I have a five-year-old sister, and I'm the only one who can take care of her. I can't go to school and raise her. The only thing I know to do is to quit school."

"My dear, what are you saying? I can only imagine what a difficult time this is for you right now, but leaving school this close to graduation is not the answer."

"What is the answer?"

"Dear, is there a relative or close friend of your parents who could help you out?"

"She has been staying with friends, but I'm afraid."

"Afraid, why afraid?"

"The Kings love her, but they don't have any children of their own, and I think they're getting too attached to her. The best way that I can honor my parents' memory is to keep us all together."

"Obviously your parents believed in your education too. I can think of no better tribute to them than the graduation they wanted for you."

"I can come back to school when Ruby is older."

"Dear, it has been my experience as an educator that few people come back. I beg you to reconsider dropping out of school. I will help you all I can. We have a student service file. Perhaps I can find someone looking for part-time work, and the funds will come from student assistance. This is not the time to be hasty. This one act could change the course of your life."

"This decision was not easy for me, and my life has already been changed. My mind is made up, Dean. This is the only way."

"Please go home and think about it more. Call me in a few days. If you feel the same, I will drop you from the class of 1949."

Pearl steeled herself for the next task; she was on her way to Sister King's. She started to call because her mother taught her to always call before visiting, but this was one time she heeded her own intuition. Deep down she felt that if she called Sister King, she would have another reason why she should not come over. When she reached the King home, Ruby was playing in the front yard with the Kings' new collie puppy, Buddy. Before Ruby came to live with them, all they talked about at church was their cute puppy and how he was their baby.

The minute Ruby saw Pearl she ran to her and hugged her knees.

"We miss you so much baby. Don't you want to come home?"

"I miss you and Diamond and Topaz. Every time I ask to go home, Sister King told me not today, maybe tomorrow."

Pearl kissed her and said, "Well, today is the day that you're coming home."

Ruby jumped up and down. "Goody, goody!" She started toward the steps to the front porch.

"Why are you going into the house?"

"To get my jacket and clothes," Ruby said. Pearl told her it was so nice and sunny, she didn't need a jacket, and she could get her clothes later.

"Let's just leave a note for Sister King so she won't worry about you." Pearl wrote a note and stuck it in the doorway, telling her that she had taken her little sister. Hand in hand they walked down the street on their way home.

Sister King was in the house fixing lunch for Ruby while she played in the front yard. Ruby and Buddy had become such good friends. Ruby added so much joy to their home. She was such a well-behaved child. Brother King called home in the middle of the day to speak to the little princess, and they both took her to the park to play with the other children. She told herself that she was doing God's work and being a good neighbor. She went to the front door with the peanut butter and jelly sandwich and the chocolate milk that Ruby loved, but she did not see her. For a moment she started to panic, but then she noticed a note on the porch floor. Slowly she bent down to retrieve the note. She recognized the handwriting before she began to read it. It was Pearl's careful script.

Sister King,

This morning I dropped out of school to take care of Ruby. There are no words to thank you for taking care of her all this time. I have taken her home, and I will pick up her clothes later. We will be forever grateful.

God bless you,
Pearl, Diamond, and Topaz

Before she finished reading, the note was wet with her tears. She dropped down on the front porch steps and called Buddy. He ran to her and sat in her lap. She buried her head in his coat and cried. She thought she should call the Morgan house to check on Ruby and Pearl, but she didn't have the heart to make the call. Once again her dream of being a mother was just that—a dream.

When Pearl and Ruby got home, Ruby was tired and so glad to be home in her own bed that she went to sleep and slept the rest of the day. Pearl was apprehensive about telling Diamond and Topaz about her decision to quit school and stay home to take care of Ruby. It affected everyone because it meant that as soon as Diamond graduated, she would have to work and support the family alone until Topaz finished nursing training. Pearl was firm in her resolve that they should support, nurture, and survive as a family unit without outside help, but it was her commitment; the next thing she had to do was sell this idea to her sisters.

Pearl was seated at the kitchen table when Diamond came home. Diamond went straight to the cabinet for a bowl and then to the refrigerator to make an ice cream sundae.

"Do you want some?"

Pearl shook her head no and began slowly, "I do need to talk to you about our future."

Diamond was lost in the pleasure of her ice cream. "I thought the insurance company said that the house was paid for, and we have some money left to live on."

"It's not about the insurance company," Pearl said. "I dropped out of school today. I need to be home running this house and taking care of Ruby. School will always be there."

Diamond stopped eating and stared at her.

"Pearl, you're almost finished. Why won't you let Sister King take care of Ruby until school is out?" Pearl frowned.

"I was over there, and I saw Sister King with Ruby. She was trying to keep her. You know how badly she has always wanted a child? She was growing too attached to her, and I was scared if she stayed over there much longer, we could never get her back."

Diamond now spoke through tears, "Pearl, there has to be another way. Daddy and Mama both wanted you to finish school."

"I know that, but they wanted us to stay together too. Right now I can't go to school. The family comes first." Diamond knew from experience there was no use arguing with Pearl when her mind was settled on an idea.

"How long will the money we have last?"

Pearl lowered her head and mumbled, "I can make it last until you graduate."

Diamond responded, puzzled, "And then what?"

Pearl answered very quickly, "You will have to stay here and support the family until Ruby gets old enough to go to school full time, and then I will go back and finish school." Diamond was so stunned that she started stuttering, and her tone elevated, "Pearl, that's another two years. I want to go out of town when I graduate."

Pearl gently laid her hand on Diamond's shoulder. "I know you do, but we all have to make sacrifices now."

Diamond pushed her hand from her shoulder and responded in a stern tone. "Pearl, Mama and Daddy did not want us to give up all our dreams to stay in this house and raise their child."

Pearl was upset at Diamond's attitude. "I don't believe what you just said to me. Their child is our sister. We are the only family she has, and we are responsible for her. It's not her fault that she lost her parents."

"Pearl, I'm not blaming anyone. We have all lost our parents. But does one tragedy just have to keep going?"

Pearl was unmoved. "I don't know why you can't see we don't have a choice in this. We have nobody to take care of Ruby. We are the only people who can do it."

Diamond picked up her half-eaten ice cream and put it in the sink. With her back to Pearl, she spoke through gritted teeth, "I can't speak for Topaz, but I think we need to call Aunt Inez and Uncle James and ask them to help you out. Ruby's life is not the only one that has changed around here." She walked out the back door, slammed it, and sat on the back steps.

Pearl came to the doorway with tears in her eyes; once again she tried to reason with her. "Diamond, it wasn't easy for me to give up school. I wanted to graduate and go out dancing with Leon Finny. More than anyone I know how badly you want to leave home. I am not picking on you or trying to take your life away. I'm just begging you to put it on hold for a little while until things are stable around here."

Diamond did not look at her she simply said, "I need some time to be alone. Is that okay? I just lost my parents, and now you're asking me to bury my dreams too."

Pearl started to say something else, but Diamond stopped her before she could say anything. "Please, Pearl, leave me alone."

Pearl went into the house and started to cook dinner. She was stunned by Diamond's reaction. Why was she only thinking about herself at a time like this? Ruby was only a little girl. They had been blessed to have their parents all this time, something Ruby would never experience. Maybe when she talked to Topaz she could make her understand that there was no other choice.

The telephone rang and interrupted her thoughts. Bishop King was snarling on the other end.

"Pearl? Yes, this is Bishop King."

"I know, sir."

"I need to know why you felt the need to steal Ruby away from our house like a thief in the night."

"A thief, Ruby is my...

"Sister King almost fainted when she went to the yard and Ruby was gone. She is—we—are trying to be helpful to all of you. I know you lost your parents, but remember, we're in grief also. Shelton and Mae are—were—our oldest friends. Both of them stood shoulder to shoulder with us at Jones when we were trying to expand from a storefront. Did you know that Sister King helped Mae pick out your name?

"No, I didn't."

"I know you didn't, but hear me, good girl. Your parents would not approve of the way you treated Sister King today. She was in the bed crying when I got home. This is not good, Pearl, not at all.

Pearl cleared her throat quietly but firmly, "Bishop King, since we lost Daddy and Mama, I'm head of the family, and I think the best place for Ruby is to stay in the house where she was born surrounded by her things, with her sisters. That's one change she won't have to adjust to. Please apologize to Sister King for me. I'm cooking dinner right now. I'll see you Sunday. Goodbye, Bishop."

"Good bye, Pearl. Think about what I said."

She got a big glass of water and tried to refocus on dinner. She didn't dare call Diamond in from the back porch to help her. She wanted to make meatloaf, but she didn't know how. She needed a cookbook, but Mama never used a cookbook. She just used a pinch of this and a cup of that and everything came out just right. She forgot about the meatloaf and made some spaghetti instead. It was easy, and everybody liked it.

Topaz was staying after class to join a study group. When she was out of school, she fell behind in her anatomy class, and she needed to take a makeup test next week. So she and three other students decided to form a study group called the "Anatomanics." Before she went to the study hall, she stopped by the pay telephone to call home. Pearl picked up the phone on the first ring.

"I'm not going to be home for dinner. I'll probably get something to eat across the street from school."

"I just thought that you'd be home tonight."

"I have to study, Pearl. I've lost so much time at school. I need extra study to keep up."

"I know, but a family matter has come up here, and I was counting on you to see my point of view."

"What kind of family matter? If it's that important tell me now."

"No you go study. The phone isn't the place to open this up. We'll talk about it when you get home."

"Bye."

When she hung up the telephone she was mildly curious, but she dismissed it, because after the loss of her parents, any other news was trivial.

Dinner was quiet; nobody talked but Ruby. She chatted on and on about Buddy and how she wished they had a puppy.

"Buddy is the cutest puppy in the world. Sister King rings a bell, and he comes every time. He's so smart, and he loves me the best. When I was over Sister King's house, he went to sleep next to my bed every night."

"Ruby?"

"Yes, Pearl?"

"Stop talking so much and eat your dinner before it gets cold."

"I'm not hungry."

"If you eat all your dinner, maybe, just maybe, we can go to the animal shelter on Saturday and look for a puppy."

"A puppy like Buddy?"

"Yes, we will look for a puppy like Buddy."

"I want one with a bushy tail."

"We will see, but first, eat." Ruby began to suck the spaghetti through her teeth. Diamond snarled, "Make her stop, Pearl. That's disgusting."

Pearl shot back. "You're the teacher. You make her stop."

"You're her mother, remember? That's your job." Pearl ignored her, and directed her attention to Ruby.

"Here, baby, let me cut your spaghetti up for you so it will be easier to eat."

For the rest of dinner Diamond was silent until she asked, "Where's Topaz?"

"She called me and said she had to stay at school to study. She'll be home late."

After dinner, to avoid Pearl, Diamond gave Ruby her bath and put her to bed. After Ruby was in bed she went straight to her room and closed the door.

It was after ten p.m. when Topaz came home. As usual Pearl was up. She didn't sleep much these days. Topaz was startled when she opened the door and Pearl spoke in the darkness, "You must be tired. It's very late."

"Yeah, time got away from us. The test is Friday, and we want to be prepared. What did you want to talk to me about on the phone? It sounded so urgent."

Pearl hesitated. "We don't need to talk tonight. You've been up all day, so get some rest, and we'll talk about it tomorrow. I really want to talk to you and Diamond together since this involves the whole family."

"My God, Pearl, you're making this bigger and bigger. What is it? Tell me right now."

"I went to get Ruby today from Sister King."

"Is that all?"

"Let me finish. Before I went to get her, I dropped out of school for good."

Topaz put her books on the coffee table. "For good? You only have four more months. Why would you drop out now?"

"Because there's no one else to take care of Ruby. She's our little sister, and we are responsible for her." Topaz moved closer to Pearl and put her arm around her.

"Pearl, you're such a special person. Mama and Daddy would be so proud."

Pearl continued, "That's not the end of it. I'm going to stay home, but you and Diamond will have to financially support the family until Ruby gets older and I can go back and finish school."

Topaz never skipped a beat. "Pearl, if you can give up your graduation, it is such a small thing to ask us to supply money. That's the easiest thing to give."

"But it also means that you'll have to stay home longer."

Topaz smiled. "Diamond is the one that wants to go to Alaska. I just want to go to bed."

Pearl kissed her on the cheek. "You're a good sister, and I wish Diamond was that easy."

"Don't worry, Pearl. I'll talk to her. She gets mad quick, but she settles down quicker. Everything will be all right." Topaz hung her jacket in the hall closet and went upstairs to bed. The light was still on, and Diamond was lying in the bed staring at the ceiling. When Topaz opened the door, she spoke without looking at her.

"Hello, late freight. I thought you got kidnapped by a night rider."

"No, I wasn't doing anything that adventurous. I was just trying to study to get a passing grade in anatomy. Did Pearl tell you she quit school today?

Diamond sat up in bed.

"Four months to go, and she bails. That must be some kind of record."

"She told me why she felt she had to quit."

For the first time Diamond faced her. "Yeah, yeah, yeah, to be Ruby's mother. You don't get a baby C.O.D. The usual way is to get married and get pregnant, but then Pearl was never too bright in biology."

Topaz began to take off her clothes. "I can't talk to you when you're in this nasty mood. Pearl did what she had to do, and we'll do what we have to do."

Diamond was defiant. "When I get my teaching certificate, I'm leaving home."

Topaz did not react to her attitude. "Time will tell. I'm turning off the lights now so that I can get some sleep. Good night, Diamond."

Diamond never answered.

REVELATION

The next morning the atmosphere was still strained between Pearl and Diamond. They did not speak to each other at all during breakfast. When Diamond left for school, she hugged Ruby and said goodbye but didn't say anything to Pearl. Diamond avoided eye contact with Topaz because she did not want to discuss it, mainly because she was sure that Topaz agreed with Pearl, and she did not feel like justifying her stand. She knew that Topaz would make her feel like a selfish, self-centered, spoiled brat.

"Diamond, have a good day. Make them see how lucky they are to have you. I have to go. I'm running late."

Pearl cleaned up the kitchen and dressed Ruby and walked her to school. On the way to school, Ruby skipped and sang. Pearl watched her skip and jump, and she was glad that the changes at home and to their lives had not affected her, at least on the outside. When she dropped Ruby off Pearl went by her aunt Inez's house to tell her about the situation at home. Diamond was so sure that she would help out with Ruby; she was determined to prove to her sister and herself that they were the only family that Ruby could depend on.

Aunt Inez only lived a mile from the school, and the walk was just what she needed to clear her head and organize her thoughts. When she knocked on the front door, nobody answered. She went around to the side door, which her aunt and uncle always kept open. As soon as she entered the house, she heard Aunt Inez humming in the backyard. She watched her from the kitchen window; she was hanging up fresh laundry on the clothesline. Watching Aunt Inez hum and hang clothes instantly brought tears to Pearl's eyes. From this angle she reminded her so much of Mama that Pearl had to turn away.

She went to the sink to get a glass of water, but the tap water was so warm that she almost spit it out. She opened the refrigerator to see if she could find a pitcher of cold water. The refrigerator was so packed with food that there was no room for a pitcher.

Pearl jumped when she heard the kitchen door slam. Aunt Inez came into the kitchen with the empty clothes-basket. When she saw Pearl she dropped the basket on the floor and hugged her so tight she almost squeezed the life out of her.

"Baby, how are you doing? Me and James was talking about you girls the other night. It's still so painful to even think about Shelton and Mae. They both just lived for their jewels." She now cupped Pearl's chin in her hand. "I want you to know that we are always here for you girls."

Pearl pulled away from her tight embrace and sat down at the kitchen table. She took a deep breath before she spoke. She had practiced her speech on the way over, but as she began to speak, her voice filled with emotion and began to quiver.

"Auntie Inez, I quit school yesterday."

Inez looked at her in amazement. "Baby, why?"

Pearl pushed forward. "Sister King she...she..."

Inez was even more puzzled. "Sister King what?"

Pearl started again. "Sister King was trying to take Ruby from us, and I didn't feel that I had a choice." By this time Pearl was openly crying. Aunt Inez pulled a dishtowel from the sink and began to wipe her eyes.

"Baby, get it all out. You've been so strong. You need these tears."

Pearl's words came out in a flood now. "Diamond says I should never have quit school, that Daddy and Mama wanted me to graduate. She said that I was letting them both down. She told me that if I asked you and Uncle James, you would keep Ruby until I finish school."

Aunt Inez used the same dishtowel and began frantically wiping off the kitchen table. She spoke without looking Pearl in the eyes.

"Baby, I wish with all my heart I could keep that sweet child, but my arthritis is acting up real bad. Most days it is almost eleven before my fingers move right. I told Mae, bless her sweet, dear soul, when she had that baby late in life that it was going to be hard to raise her. I'm three years older than Mae. I just don't have the energy to keep a young child, especially one that is as spirited as Ruby."

"Auntie Inez, it would only be until I graduate, and I would come over here every day straight from school, and we could take her home on the weekend. I just want her to be with family."

Aunt Inez finally faced her and talked to her in a counseling tone. "Pearl, you are young, but you still grown. Some girls your age have children already. Sometimes in life things happen that we cannot control. I'm sorry you had to drop out of school, but, baby, you still got enough schooling to get you a good job. When I first started working, I cleaned white folks' houses. Thanks to Shelton and Mae, that's something you girls will never have to do. James and me can help with money if you run short, but we can't take on Ruby. Next month we going down to Arkansas to visit James's sister. We might be gone for a month. We have raised our kids. This is our time to do what we want to do."

Pearl apologized. "I only asked you because Diamond was so sure that you would keep her. She does not want to stay home after graduation."

Aunt Inez put both hands on her hips and stamped her foot. "Diamond is going to have to learn that she has to put her family first in times of need just like everybody else. You two are the oldest. She has got to stand with you in this. It's all part of being a woman. I'll talk to her if you want me to." She opened the refrigerator and started moving the food around. "You hungry, baby? I made a good pot roast last night. Let me fix you a big 'ole sandwich. You always loved my pot roast when you were little."

Pearl shrugged her shoulders, "No, Auntie Inez, I'm full."

Diamond could not concentrate; every class was a blur. She had been raised in church all her life. She was taught that God was just and fair to those who obeyed him. Her father and mother lived, loved, worshiped, and obeyed to the best of their abilities. Why had God done this to them?

Her Sunday school teacher always told her to accept without question, but hard as she tried, she could not accept this. When Pearl asked her to stay home after graduation, it was like a steel vice tightening around her head. More than anything, she wanted freedom. She loved her family, but she wanted to go to new places with strange names, places like Tahiti and Madrid, and meet new people. She knew every street in Detroit like the back of her hand, and she felt that there was so much more, maybe in California or New York.

Everybody here just went to work and back home and on Sunday, church. She wanted to see a real play on stage like the ones she read about in the movie magazines, and spend New Year's Eve in Times Square—things Pearl didn't even think about. Pearl's vision was so limited and her expectations so small that Diamond couldn't even begin to explain her dreams to her. There was no use talking to Topaz either, because she and Pearl thought with one brain. She did feel sorry for Ruby, but she didn't believe that harm would come to her staying with Bishop and Sister King. She was sure that was what her mama and daddy would have wanted. Pearl was being overly dramatic. If push came to shove, Sister King had no legal rights to Ruby.

When her classes ended, she went to the library. If she waited until six p.m., Topaz would be home, and she would not be forced to communicate with Pearl. When Diamond got off the bus, Topaz was standing at the bus stop waiting for her.

Three buses had passed, and she was about to give up when she saw Diamond. Diamond started to walk the other way, but Topaz grabbed her arm before she could get away. Diamond was not accustomed to Topaz being this aggressive, and she was slightly thrown off guard. Topaz was adamant. "We need to talk."

"There is nothing to talk about. I'm not going to change my mind. If Pearl wants to be a heroine, that's up to her. I have plans for my time and life."

Topaz stopped and looked her straight in the eye. "We all had plans, but when we lost Daddy and Mama, plans have to change whether we like it or not. Let's go to the park and discuss this."

The park was two blocks from the bus stop, and Diamond walked a full foot behind Topaz. When they got to the park, Topaz led her to a bench in the corner of the park that had the least foot traffic. As she began, Diamond was amazed. She had never seen Topaz speaking with such passion, authority, and confidence. Topaz had matured in the last weeks from a girl to a woman. At first it was hard to listen to her because she could not stop looking at her. Diamond was afraid that Topaz was not strong enough to be a nurse, but after watching her take charge, she knew all her fears were groundless.

Topaz's words were a symphony of compassion and love. She cajoled, reasoned, and cried with Diamond; she did not belittle her dreams or think they were in the least bit frivolous.

"Diamond, I know more than anybody how much you want to leave Detroit. We sleep in the same room, and night after night I have listened to you talk about the faraway places you want to visit after you graduate. I'm so sad that it seems like your dreams are vanishing. They are not gone. Just delayed." Her voice was shaking as she wiped tears away.

"Nobody could have predicted the hurt and pain we're all going through. Pearl feels that she owes it to Mama and Daddy to take care of Ruby. Right or wrong, that's the way she feels and we can't change her. I love you both, and I want to bring some peace to this situation. When I finish my training, you can pack your bags and say so long to Detroit forever. With my nursing degree, I'll be able to support us. Who knows by that time Pearl will probably be tired of washing and ironing anyway." She squeezed Diamond's hand.

"Do we have a deal?" Diamond kissed her on the cheek.

"We have a deal, but you tell Pearl. I love her too, but right now I don't like her very much."

Diamond and Topaz left the park in silence but nevertheless on one accord. When they walked into the house, Pearl's heart stopped when she saw them both together because she did not know what to expect. Diamond went straight upstairs without speaking, still leaving Pearl in the dark. Topaz waited until Diamond was upstairs and out of ear range. Pearl could not wait for Topaz to speak. "How did it go? Is she staying home?"

"We made a deal. She'll stay until I graduate." Pearl breathed a deep sigh.

"Thank God for you. You're the only person on earth who could have gotten through to her."

"Pearl, don't talk to her about this again. Just leave her alone."

Four months later Diamond graduated with honors from Michigan State Teachers College. She delivered the valedictorian address, "Tomorrow the World," which she had worked on for over three weeks, practicing it over and over again until everybody in the house knew it by memory, and presented the dean of students with the class gift.

Her graduation dress was, for the lack of a better word, a confection. She knew that because everyone was wearing graduation gowns, they would not put any effort into their clothes. Her goal was to shock everyone when she removed her gown. She made her dress from three different patterns. One pattern for the bodice, a sweetheart neckline from a formal strapless dress pattern; another one for the three-quarter length sleeves, from a blouse pattern; and finally a form-fitting wrap skirt from a suit pattern. The dress was pale yellow silk organza with transparent chiffon sleeves. The material alone for the dress was over three dollars a yard. Pearl shook her head at the expense, but Diamond ignored her and bought it anyway. The dress was all she had hoped for—one of her classmates, Tyrone Evans, said she looked like a cool glass of lemonade walking.

When she received her degree, she had her own private cheering section. Uncle James put Ruby on his shoulders so that she could get a good view. Although she was thrilled to be the first college graduate in the family, she also felt a wave of sadness wash over her because her parents could not share this happiness with her. After graduation Uncle James pulled out all the stops and took them all to the Golden Door, one of the most expensive Negro restaurants in Detroit, and Uncle James ordered pressed duck for everyone. Ruby entertained the entire restaurant doing duck imitations. The food was delicious. Topaz surprised everyone with an uncharacteristic toast.

"Glasses up, everybody. This is a wonderful day. We're surrounded by loved ones here and in heaven to salute our sister's achievement: the first Morgan to earn a sheepskin. She's the head of her class and as smart as she is beautiful. Diamond, like your name, you're full of sparkle. You almost glow in the dark."

Diamond was so touched that she openly cried. The day was full and rich, and for a short time, laughing and talking with family was like old times.

Diamond's student teaching position began two weeks after her graduation. She was placed in a fifth-grade classroom at Clark Elementary School. Clark was an old school with a good academic reputation. It was large and covered the entire block of a middle-class Negro neighborhood. The school had three floors, a large gym, a full auditorium, and a fully equipped teacher's lounge. Of the school's faculty, only four teachers were Negro. Diamond was assigned to work with Mr. Michael Ramsey, the head math teacher.

When Mr. Mangus, their principal, introduced them Diamond was shocked. She was shaking hands with one of the most handsome men she had ever seen. She was sure if she looked up "tall, dark, and handsome," she would find his picture.

When the students began to file into the room, the boys did a double take when they were introduced to Miss Morgan, who was going to working with them this semester. Diamond thought that she would be nervous in front of her first classroom, but surprisingly, she was comfortable with the students.

Diamond came home singing from her day at school. It was the first time in a month that Pearl had even seen her civil. Diamond's attitude was still chilly, but today she spoke. Without being asked she even helped Pearl with the laundry. When Topaz got home she was bubbling over with news about her day and Michael Ramsey, the most handsome Negro she had ever seen. She loved the kids and how good it felt to finally be an independent woman. Topaz hung on her every word. Pearl couldn't help it, but when she heard her joy, she was a bit jealous of the closeness that Diamond and Topaz shared. They both admired and loved Pearl, but they really liked each other. Mae had been Pearl's best friend, and she didn't build the same bond with Diamond or Topaz. Now she so badly needed a friend, she regretted it. She cuddled Ruby closer as she slept and kissed her and vowed that she would always be the sister to her that she longed for.

The days went into weeks, and the weeks became months, which slowly turned into years. The Morgan sisters' lives became a permanent routine. Pearl cooked, cleaned, and mothered Ruby. She threw herself into church work with a vengeance. She did not ever go back to school or speak of it again.

Pearl's whole life centered on the home. Her next-door neighbor was her only close lady friend outside of the family. Evelyn and Joe Cobb lived next door with their young son, Joe Jr. Evelyn was nosy and bossy, but Pearl was grateful for the company and ignored her faults. The Cobbs' son became a playmate for Ruby. Evelyn and Pearl grocery shopped together and spent time talking over the back fence that joined their houses. Evelyn dutifully followed Pearl to church; she joined Jones Tabernacle a year later. She immediately decided to become a member of the Young Adult Choir; her self-esteem soared as everyone complimented her strong alto voice. Pearl was the go-to person for every committee and auxiliary at church; she was the youngest trustee member in the history of Jones Tabernacle. She was so reliable that Bishop King gave her the keys to the church because he knew she would be the first one there.

Diamond worked hard every day at school and won prizes for her classroom every September. Her bulletin boards were works of art, and she lovingly made white eyelet curtains for her classroom windows. She chose eyelet so that the sun could stream through the holes. She washed and starched them once a month so that they always looked brand new. She worked twice a month on Saturday at the Community Youth Center as a job counselor to earn extra money, because now Pearl insisted that Ruby needed to attend private school, and she also was in ballet and piano class. Pearl was determined that Ruby should have every advantage to make up for the loss of her parents. Diamond used to question the wisdom of this excess, but eventually she just stopped talking and signed the checks.

Diamond was the chairwoman of the Jones Tabernacle Annual Fashion Show; she designed the outfits and selected all the models. Her commentaries were tastefully written and delivered. The fashion show was so popular that twice it was outlined in the Black Society pages of the *Detroit Register Newspaper*, where she was praised as a "Diamond in the rough."

She dated Michael Ramsey for two years and was hopeful that it would blossom into a commitment. Michael cared for her deeply, but he was anxious to have a family. He felt that she was too enmeshed with her sisters, and her obligations were too demanding. So they drifted apart, and she watched with quiet desperation and simmering rage at the cards that life had dealt her when he married a soft-spoken sales clerk who worked at Woolworth's Drugstore. She swallowed hard and buried her feelings again when eight years later his daughter, Rose—named for his mother—was one of her third grade students. She finally realized that her life was set and that her moment to escape had passed.

Topaz quickly climbed the ladder at Good Shepherd Hospital. Good Shepherd was a private, small 600-bed facility; a small hospital where excellence would not go unnoticed. When she graduated she had been accepted at Henry Ford Hospital; it was a bigger hospital with more prestige, but she could not bear to work where her father and mother had died. Mrs. Wright, the supervisor of nurses at Good Shepherd, was impressed with her clinical skills but awed by the innate empathy and compassion that she displayed as she cared for her patients. Mrs. Wright purposely assigned her to the wing with the terminal patients because she knew that Topaz was a beacon of light that could shatter the darkness of their conditions.

She would sit with them, read to them, and listen to them without ever seeming to tire. Topaz was born to be a nurse. She gave so much of herself to her patients that many nights she came home and went straight to bed. She did not have the energy to participate in family functions or many outside activities. On the rare occasion when she was free, Diamond would convince her to go to a movie. As hard as she tried to enjoy the movie as much as Diamond, she would always fall asleep before the movie was over, and Diamond had to recreate the end for her on the way home. Topaz was always amazed at how clearly Diamond remembered every word of dialogue and what the actors wore and how the scenery and music was perfect for the picture. Listening to Diamond was always more entertaining than the movie.

Life stayed the same for Pearl, Diamond, and Topaz as Ruby turned from a little girl to a primary school student and a pre-teen. She had been a pretty little girl, but as she grew, her prettiness intensified and turned into loveliness. She was petite and possessed a doll-like figure. She had beautiful eyes and full lips that were a trademark of the Morgan family. Her hair, though not as luxurious as Diamond's, was thick and full, and she was the only sister who inherited their mother's red color. She had a standing two-week appointment at Laura's Beauty Shop. While all little girls her age wore braids, Ruby's hair was curled and styled with her trademark cut bangs. Laura used her as a model to lure customers, claiming that she colored her hair. Diamond and Topaz protested because they had only been to the beauty shop after they were grown and working, but Pearl insisted that Ruby's hair was so thick that it needed to be done professionally. Pearl was obsessive in her quest to shower Ruby with things; she would not listen to reasonable arguments about the subject. Ruby had to have the best.

Diamond and Topaz worked and made the money that Pearl managed and spent on Ruby. Pearl spoiled Ruby with things, and she did not discipline her and would not tolerate any interference with her authority when it related to Ruby. Pearl's whole world revolved around Ruby; she drove her to school and to her dance lessons and piano classes. On Sundays Pearl took Ruby to church and played the piano for the young people's choir where Ruby was a member. Her voice was not the greatest, but Pearl insisted that she get some solo parts. The congregation always politely clapped when she finished, and the usual comments were, "She tries hard." Family and church members tried in vain to warn Pearl about the danger of raising Ruby to think that everything in life should be given to her without responsibility. Pearl politely listened and promptly ignored all their advice, because time had eased but not erased the memory of a five-year-old child lifted up to two caskets to kiss her parents goodbye.

RENEWAL

Bishop King was getting older, and he feared that his days might be numbered. He did not want to leave Jones Tabernacle without a shepherd. Sister King was not well, and he was spending more and more time nursing her at home. He recruited a young assistant pastor, William Barnes, and a young deacon, Oscar Pelt, to help him shoulder the duties of the everyday running of the church.

William was a bright, eager young minister with the energy that Bishop King was looking for. His best asset was his charismatic wife; she charmed all the parishioners with her sparking personality. She was the perfect mate for William. He was a quiet and introspective man, and her outgoing ways complemented him perfectly. She started having luncheons at her home for the church committees and was the director of the vacation Bible school. She could always be heard before she was seen. She was all over the church, and her persona was so different from Sister King's—who was passive and always deferred to her husband—that she was a welcome change and a blast of fresh air.

Sister Barnes and Pearl naturally gravitated toward one another. Pearl, along with the rest of the congregation, was intrigued with this powerhouse. Evelyn had been Pearl's only friend, but slowly she and Sister Barnes became in Zula Barnes's words, "play sisters." Pearl gradually drifted from Evelyn and began to spend all her free time with Sister Barnes.

Another surprising addition to Pearl's life was Deacon Pelt. Pearl could not help but notice how he always managed to sit next to her in the trustee meeting or make sure he walked her to the car and mentioned how tastefully she dressed. Oscar Pelt was the son of a long line of Baptist preachers. His family had migrated from Memphis, Tennessee, like so many other Negros in the 1940s seeking a better financial future. He was the youngest son of three brothers; he was tall, dark, and handsome. All the available single women of the church swooned over him; they simply could not do enough for him. He was bombarded with homemade cookies, sweet potato pies, and peach cobblers. The older sisters were always inviting him to dinner to meet a cousin or a niece. Deacon Pelt was very gracious in accepting this adoration but declined to date any of the baking queens. He was smitten with Pearl and admired the regal way she carried herself. She was not flirtatious or aggressive, and that made him more determined to win her affection. She was so busy with home and Ruby she did not even think about a mate. She was aware that Deacon Pelt was the catch of the church and assumed that he would eventually marry one of the eager sisters. In an effort to be closer to Pearl, he joined the choir. He endured the teasing about how weak his voice was and pretended to not hear the whispers about him being tone deaf.

"Pearl, do you ever visit other churches?"

"No, Jones is my home church. Why would I feel the need to go somewhere else? I play every Sunday morning. What would the choir do if I wasn't there?

"The same thing they would if you were sick. Sister Conley would have to take over. I know you're Jones born and bred, but sometimes it helps to see other services."

"I don't understand what you mean."

"Bishop King is an old-time religion preacher, which is not bad, but my father's church is progressive, and maybe we could get some new ideas from the service. If nothing else, maybe some new song choices for the choir."

"What's wrong with the choir?"

"Nothing, Pearl, it's just the old spirituals are outdated now. Just come with me and see the difference. If you bring new ideas back to Jones, everyone will say you're a woman of vision."

The date was set for the second Sunday, a quiet one at Jones, to visit Friendship Baptist Church. Pearl did not tell Diamond or Topaz, opting instead to meet him at the church. She chose to let Evelyn be in charge of Ruby. She was nervous and dressed with particular care. She was determined not to treat this as a date but simply as two church friends spending an afternoon together.

Catching them at the door before they left for Sunday school she blurted out, "I won't be at morning service today. I'm going to another church for morning service."

As usual, Diamond was not satisfied. "Are you just telling us now? Is that why you're so dressed up today?" She moved closer.

"Pearl Morgan, I do declare you have on makeup. Have you been on my dresser?" Ruby keeping in character changed the focus to her, said, "Diamond and Topaz are going to the show after church. I don't want to be home by myself."

Pearl smiled at her. "After they leave you can go next door."

"You'll be fine. I'll call Evelyn before I leave."

"Okay, how are you going to get there? Is somebody picking you up?"

"I'll just take the bus."

Diamond laughed. "All dressed up and taking the bus."

"I would call a cab."

Topaz, already in the car, blew the horn. "Are we going to Jones this morning, or having service on the porch?"

Diamond and Ruby ran down the steps and drove off.

Pearl could not understand why she felt the need to conceal the truth from Diamond, Topaz, and Ruby. She did know that the thought of this little secret white lie made her feel giddy. When Pearl got off the bus in front of the church, Oscar was waiting for her.

"When you called me and asked me to meet you at the bus stop, I couldn't believe it. Why in heavens name did you take the bus?"

"My sisters needed the car to get to church. There are three of them and only one of me. The majority wins."

Oscar continued to scold. "I know where you live. It would have been a pleasure to pick you up."

"I know that, but to tell the truth, I'm so nervous about meeting your father, the ride was good for my butterflies." Oscar spoke of his father with great respect, and she knew that his opinion of her was crucial.

Reverend Pelt Sr. was a widower; he lost his wife when Oscar was thirteen, and he raised him alone from that point. Oscar playfully scolded her about the cloak-and-dagger attitude and not letting him pick her up and drive her to the church. He assured her that his father would love her. Before she could respond, his father walked up. Pastor Pelt was an older version of his son; he was tall and stately, sophisticated with salt and pepper gray hair. When he spoke he revealed pearly white teeth.

"Son, is this the young woman you were so eager for me to meet?"

"Yes, Dad. This is Miss Pearl Morgan, the life and blood of Jones Tabernacle Church. Pearl, this is my father, Pastor Oscar Pelt Senior." The elder Pelt shook her hand. It was a firm handshake.

"Son, you didn't tell me that she was so attractive. Pearl is the right name for you. You're a gem."

Pearl blushed. Oscar was surprised; this was the first time he had witnessed a chink in Pearl's armor.

"Dad, don't steal her away from me. Give me a chance to make her smile."

"My son speaks about your dedication to your church with so much admiration. I know your parents must be proud. Most times an apple doesn't fall far from the tree. They must be hardworking Christian soldiers on the LORD's battlefield."

"Years ago, well when I was twenty, both my parents were instantly killed in a car accident. My father was ill, and they were on the way to a drugstore to get him some medicine, and their car was run off the road by a hit-and-run driver."

He looked straight in her eyes as he softly spoke, "What you need, young lady, is a strong man." With this statement he winked to his son. "Which should be no problem for you." To Pearl's amazement she enjoyed this attention and flattery.

All day long Oscar introduced her to the church members. She met the deaconess, the mothers of the church, the usher board, and the choir. With each introduction he became more and more possessive. He held her hand, put his arm around her shoulder, and pulled out her chair at dinner after service. Pearl was so nervous and excited she barely touched her food. His father's sermon was very moving; the lesson was to love the unlovable. When service was over, Pearl waited until she could steal a minute alone with Pastor Pelt.

"I enjoyed your message so much. I felt as though you were speaking directly to me. I looked around, and the whole congregation was moved."

He kissed her on the cheek. "You make an old man feel good. I want you to visit us again soon. I know you have a church home, but I want you to consider us your second home." She started to walk away, and he whispered in her ear. "From the day he was born, we raised Oscar Jr. to take over this pulpit when I retire, which could be as soon as he starts his own family."

She was still blushing when Oscar led her outside to his car and opened the passenger side for her. "No, Oscar, the bus stop is right on the next corner. It's such a nice day. I don't mind."

"Pearl what is all this hide-and-seek about? I don't have a girlfriend or wife."

"I know you're not spoken for."

"I like a mystery as well as the next person, but this doesn't make sense. At least let me drive you to your block. I can't let people see you get on the bus when my car is right here. My father will kill me."

They drove in complete silence, each lost in their own thoughts. Oscar was now determined more than ever that Pearl Morgan was going to be his wife. She had all the qualities that he desired in a mate, and more importantly the church and his father approved of her, which was a prominent factor in his decision.

"The next street coming up will be Sutton Avenue. You were right. Your father's church is lovely and more progressive than Jones. You can let me out on the corner." Before she could she get out of the car, Oscar leaned over, turned his head and tried to kiss her.

"Don't do that."

"Why?"

"For one we are in public, I grew up on this street, everybody knows me, and I don't want any gossip to start about me kissing in the car on Sunday afternoon."

Oscar laughed. "People kiss on Sunday Pearl."

"You know what I mean." She pulled away and got out of the car. Oscar was still laughing as he drove away. Pearl was thrilled that she had opened this Pandora's Box, and now she did not want to close it.

As she walked down the street, her mind and heart were racing. She had truly enjoyed this afternoon. It was a pleasant change to spend time with a chivalrous, affectionate man. These past years she had devoted all of her time to her family. She had never taken time to let herself even think for one moment of another life, and now even though she could not see how it could be possible, she let her mind drift away to the possibility that it might happen.

When she reached the house, Ruby and Joe Jr. were sitting on the Cobbs' front porch.

"Pearl, where have you been? It's almost four o clock. Pearl ignored the question.

"Is Diamond home? Did she cook dinner?"

"She cooked before they left for the movie. She left a plate for you on the stove. Everyone had somewhere to go or something to do today but me."

"Trust me, Ruby, your day will come. Let's go on in the house. Joe, thank your mother for me."

She was glad that she did not have to face Diamond and Topaz and more questions. She went into the kitchen and unwrapped the plate that Diamond left for her. Diamond was such a good cook, and her meals were so inventive that it was like opening a Christmas present. She could not wait to see what was on the plate; Diamond didn't disappoint. It was a simple menu, but the design and the color balance on the plate made it so special. On Sundays she always experimented with new recipes. Today she made stuffed pork chops with spinach and corn. Because she had been too nervous to eat in front of Oscar at church, she was starving. She ate it all.

"Well, Pearl, how did it feel to play hooky from church today?"

"Really, Diamond, I didn't miss church."

Topaz wanted to know about the service. "Do they have a good choir? How was the sermon?"

"Everything was nice, but I missed my Jones family." She quickly changed the subject. "Diamond, as always, dinner was delicious."

Pearl knew deep inside her soul why she did not want to talk about her afternoon with Oscar. As much as she hated to admit it even to herself, she was sure that she was not worthy of a complete love life. She saw herself as a person who gave service to others. Even though she was the oldest sister, she had always felt diminished by Diamond because her sister was so pretty and accomplished. She did not have her gift of coyness and witty conversation or her wonderful sense of style. That's why she kept her thoughts to herself when it came to the opposite sex. Her mother had always told her she would make some man a good wife, and she believed her, but at the same time she thought her mother would always be available when the time came to help and show her how to choose one.

Pearl was very careful not to let anyone at church see her staring at Oscar. He was always trying to steal glances, but she avoided his eyes at all times. She was astonished that Diamond did not pick up Oscar's signals because she was so sharp and insightful, but Pearl reasoned that the thought of someone being interested in her was so foreign to her that she completely missed it.

TRUST BETRAYED

One morning after Ruby left for school, Oscar called Pearl. "Can I come over?"

"Right now? Oscar it's so early, I have dishes to wash, beds to make, floors to sweep. This morning would not be a good time."

"Pearl I'm not coming to inspect the house. I need to see you. I know you're alone. Diamond and Topaz are at work, and Ruby is at school. What I have say won't wait for another time."

She was frustrated with his insistence. "Oscar what is the big emergency?"

"Pearl, I need to talk to you in person. I'm on my way." Before she could say another word, he hung up.

She began to pace up and down the kitchen floor. She and Oscar had been carrying on a secret association for the last six months. She considered it innocent, but she had to admit even to herself that it was growing in intensity.

Oscar often took her on long rides to the country in the afternoons and accompanied her to the grocery store several times. She enjoyed his company and the way he found such pleasure in just spending time with her doing everyday chores. Last Sunday after church he invited her to dinner at his father's home. Oscar's favorite aunt cooked dinner, and they treated her like a daughter. Being with family around the dinner table brought back such sweet memories of what she lost, and she did not know until that day how much she missed it. She almost cried.

She went upstairs to change from her work clothes to something nicer. She pulled off her housedress and put on a skirt and blouse. She brushed her hair and was about to look for some earrings when the doorbell rang. She checked her watch; she had only spoken to him a very short time ago. He must have taken an airplane to get there that fast. Before she could get down the bottom of the stairs, he rang the bell again; she had to call out to tell him to wait a minute that she was on her way to the door. When she opened the door, he kissed her. She was shocked as well as surprised; he had never been this bold with her before, and she was thrown completely off guard. When she was able to compose herself, she asked what made him kiss her right on her front porch. He did not explain or apologize but stepped inside the door and pulled her close to him and attempted to kiss her again. This time she pulled away and told him that he would have to go if he could not behave like a gentleman. He smiled and mocked her.

"I am a gentleman, and you are a gentlewoman, so can't we be kind to each other?" All the irritation melted away from Pearl when he smiled at her. He went on, "Can we sit? I have some great news, and I almost ran all the way over here because you are the first one I want to share it with." He was so excited that he had a hard time catching his breath. "My father called me last night and told me to get to his church fast. He had just spoken with a visiting pastor from Arkansas who is retiring at the end of the month. He is looking for a young, spirit-filled minister to awaken his stagnant congregation."

Pearl was puzzled, "What does that have to do with you?"

He shook her. "Pearl, wake up. I am the man for the job. I don't have to wait years and years for my father to retire and give me his church. God has put one right in my hands, and to put the cherry on the sundae, I have my father's blessing."

Pearl was shaken, but she tried hard to smile through her disappointment at the thought of Oscar leaving Detroit. "I am so happy for you, Oscar."

"No, you are happy for us. This is perfect. I have a church, and now I need a first lady."

"First lady?"

"You, Pearl. This is my clumsy way of asking you to be my wife and partner for the rest of my life."

Pearl almost fainted. "I have obligations. I am the only mother Ruby knows. I can't leave her."

"You don't have to leave her. She can come with us."

Pearl continued as though she didn't hear and answered him in whispered tones. "Diamond and Topaz can take care of themselves. But Ruby will have to leave her home."

"Pearl, the ministry comes with a parsonage. She will still live in her own home. I am aware of your devotion to your little sister. That is one of the reasons I care for you so deeply, your unselfish love. You would be the perfect mother to our children."

Pearl rose from the seat and walked to the kitchen. Oscar followed her.

"I'm waiting for an answer, Pearl."

"Oscar, this is so fast, and I'm so overwhelmed that there is no way I can answer today."

"Pearl, I need to know before the end of the week. I am going to tell Bishop King tonight, and Sunday at church I would like to announce our future plans."

"Oscar, we haven't even discussed our friendship with the family. I need a little time to talk to them."

"You know what we have is deeper than friendship, sweetheart. We can talk to them together. I'm sure they will be as happy for us as I am. You have wonderful sisters."

"You don't understand, Oscar. Years ago we made an agreement to stay together to raise Ruby, and then we would be free."

"Pearl, that was years ago, and life changes every day, even in the Morgan household." When she closed the door as Oscar left, her heart sank. For some reason even unknown to her, she felt this dream might be dying.

Pearl went next door to Evelyn's for no other reason than at this moment she did not want to be alone. When she walked in the house, Evelyn was ironing.

"Where are you coming from? You look like you just left a fashion show at Hudson's."

Pearl ignored her question and started to sprinkle the shirts on the table.

"What's wrong, Pearl? You look like you have the weight of the world on your shoulders."

"Nothing's wrong. I just feel a little out of sorts today."

"There is a box of baking soda on the top shelf. You know baking soda will cure anything. If that don't work, take some of that castor oil. You probably just need to go to the bathroom."

Pearl came over to try to tell Evelyn about her and Oscar, but somehow the words would not come. They spent the entire afternoon together talking about this and that and a whole lot of nothing.

Evelyn loved discussing her marriage with Pearl because she felt this was the one area in which she was superior. She delighted in telling her about the nice things that Joe said to her or the unexpected gift he brought home last week for no apparent reason.

Because Pearl could feel her glee in upstaging her, she was almost tempted to tell her that she had a marriage proposal earlier this morning, but the words stuck in her throat.

Topaz had a rare opportunity to break away from the hospital for lunch. Usually she was so busy that she worked straight shifts until she went home, but today a new class of nurse interns invaded the hospital, and the halls were running over with eager new caregivers. She and her supervisor, Della Cole, decided to treat themselves to Chinese food for lunch. The restaurant was just around the corner from the hospital; they giggled like schoolgirls who were playing hooky from school. When they got the menu they didn't know what to order. The dishes were foreign to them, and the waiter's broken English was so hard to understand that they just gave up and ordered chop suey.

While they were waiting for their order, Oscar and Reverend Barnes came into the restaurant. William Barnes spotted Topaz before she saw him and walked behind her and put his hands over her eyes.

"Guess who?" he said jokingly.

Topaz put her hands over his and joined in the joke.

"I am a genie who can make you disappear if you don't identify these hands this instant." William playfully, quickly snatched his hands from her eyes.

"Deacon Pelt, God knew we were needed here to banish this demon from Sister Morgan's soul."

"Della Taylor, these two handsome young men are members of my church, Oscar Pelt and William Barnes. Oscar is on the deacon board, and William is one of our assistant pastors. We are in anointed company today. I know you're going to join us for lunch?"

"This is our day, Deacon Pelt."

"Thank the LORD, Reverend Barnes." Topaz and Della looked on in amazement as they ordered without the menu. When the waitress came to the table, William ordered in his pastoral cadence. "The china express special, please." He got impatient when Oscar hesitated. "Speak, brother."

"Just a minute, Reverend. I'll just get my usual won ton soup, extra hot. You ladies order whatever you want. Lunch is on Reverend Barnes."

Oscar was unusually animated and barely touching his food. Topaz asked him why he was so talkative. He told them about the offer to go to Arkansas and how pleased he was to be given this vote of confidence so early in his ministry. Topaz assured him that he surely deserved this and how much the Jones Tabernacle family would miss him. He told her the only down side to this whole advancement was leaving Jones, but he felt he was gaining a new family both spiritually and personally, and he felt blessed. Della was curious about the two-fold blessing. He hedged at first, but then he joyously told them that he had proposed marriage this morning and was very expectant that he would soon be a married. Topaz was astonished. She was frantically trying to mentally place which sister at church had caught this prize fish. All eyes at the table were facing him now. William was the first one to speak.

"Well, you are a sly one. Speak up, brother. Is it someone from your father's church? If it isn't, I need to know before Sunday so I can clear my calendar to make room to counsel all the brokenhearted single women at our church."

Oscar regretted that he had revealed too much and began to backpedal. "I guess it would be proper to wait until the lady says yes before I start advertising."

William began to tease him saying, "Brother, you don't drop a bomb like that without picking up the pieces." Topaz almost choked, between sips of water she stammered. "Oscar who is she? Somebody at Jones?" Della asked.

"Who's the lucky girl?"

Oscar hedged. "Like I said, the engagement isn't official yet. I'm waiting and still praying for her answer."

Della pushed. "Why talk about it then? You didn't even have to bring it up if you were just going to tease us."

Oscar, avoiding everyone's eyes at the table, simply said. "My mistake."

The meal continued in silence until Della spoke. "Topaz we better get back to work. Our time is almost up."

As the men rose, Topaz stopped while Della waited at the door. "This is not over, Deacon. Thanks for the lunch, William. It was a good break in the day."

To make up for his slip of the tongue, as he put it, he picked up the bill and paid for everyone's lunch.

"I know you left a good tip for the waitress since I paid the bill."

William looked him straight in the eye and said, "I took care of the waitress, brother, but my tip for you today is not to keep secrets from your best friend."

Topaz was preoccupied all day with the news of Oscar's marriage. Ever since the first day he arrived at Jones Tabernacle, the single women's membership had been taking bets on which one he would court. It was always strange to everyone that despite his courteous manner and charming personality he never really appeared to favor any one woman in the church. He made it clear that the lady in question was not a member of his father's church, so that meant it was somebody that they all knew. Topaz's mind was like a jigsaw puzzle as she desperately tried to piece together church services or events where she could remember Oscar paying special attention to one person. As hard as she tried to jog her memory the answer still eluded her. Eventually she stopped trying to figure it out and concentrated on another thought; she could not wait to get home to tell Pearl and Diamond.

The dinner table was always Diamond's stage; she held court telling one story after another, about school or some teacher or something interesting she had read in the newspaper. Tonight she was going to steal the spotlight; she planned how she was going to announce the news after dinner but before dessert. She would casually tell them about the unexpected pleasure of bumping into William Barnes and Oscar Pelt at lunch today. She would mention that during the lunch Oscar told her that he was engaged, and then she would nonchalantly leave the table. She smiled to herself because she could hardly wait to see the looks of shock on Pearl and Diamond's faces as they raced behind her to hear the whole story. Tonight the curtain was going up on her opening act, and Diamond was going to be an understudy.

Pearl left Evelyn's house to go home to start dinner. She didn't have to pick up Ruby because she had cheerleading practice after school, and the coach always brought the girls home after practice. She made dinner in a zombie state; she opened the refrigerator, walked to the stove, and set the table all without remembering how each task was done until it was completed. She quietly thanked God for not letting her cut or burn herself when the dinner was done.

Diamond was the first one to get home because school ended at three thirty p.m. She briefly spoke to Pearl and went upstairs to change clothes, telling Pearl how she had to hurry up and get out of her stockings because her legs were hot. While she was upstairs she decided to take a quick, cool bath. She had recess duty this week, and the schoolyard was hot. The children running back and forth made the gravel fly, and the dust was still sticking to her skin. She loved to teach, but mundane tasks such as hall and lunchroom duties were not courses that were covered in her degree program. She felt they were nonprofessional functions. When she voiced this opinion in teacher's meetings, her principal said those assignments fell under "other duties as assigned," and the school budget did not allow for extra employees to cover part-time positions. And besides, she was the only teacher that complained. So she learned to shut up and gritted her teeth as the gravel flew around her.

After she came out of the bathroom feeling like a new person, she decided that she would skip dinner at home and go downtown to Famous and Barr, do some window shopping, and maybe grab a hamburger and Coke at Woolworth's lunch counter.

"I'll see you later, Pearl."

"Diamond, where are you going? I'm just putting dinner on the table."

"Not for me. I'll grab something while I'm out."

"Why would you spend money eating when food is ready right here? That's just silly. Are you meeting someone?"

"I have to go. See you when I get back. Goodbye Pearl."

This was one day she was not in the mood to remind her that she was Ruby's mother; her mother Mae was gone to glory resting in heaven.

Pearl was setting the table when Topaz came flying through the front door, out of breath and talking a mile a minute. "Pearl, you will never believe what happened today. Where's Diamond? I want to tell you both together."

"Who knows where Diamond is? She just walked out of the house with no explanation of where she was going and how long she would be there. When I asked her, she acted like she didn't hear me, as usual. She can be so moody sometimes. I'm not going to hold dinner for her. Tonight it's just you and me. Ruby will be home later after practice, and I'll put her plate aside."

Topaz was crestfallen; there was no way she was going to be able to hold her news until Diamond decided to come home. She began to walk behind Pearl so closely that when Pearl turned abruptly, she bumped into her.

"Topaz, what is it? I'm going to sit down and let you tell me your news. Is this better? You have my undivided attention." Pearl took a chair and sat quietly while Topaz recounted the story. She began by telling Pearl that she and her friend went to a Chinese restaurant for lunch and ran into Oscar Pelt and William Barnes. This piqued Pearl's interest.

"What time was it when you saw them?"

"We left the hospital about two p.m., so it must have been a little over. Anyway what difference does it make what time it was?"

"No difference. I was just asking."

"Stop cutting in. Let me get to the good part. Oscar told us that he proposed to his ladylove today and that when they get married, they're going to move to Arkansas where he's going to be the pastor of a new church. My mind was working overtime today trying to place him with every single woman in church, but I kept coming up empty."

Pearl spoke aloud her inner thoughts before she had time to think and momentarily forgot Topaz was even in the room.

"He promised he wouldn't say anything until we talked about it again."

Topaz was stunned. She looked at Pearl in disbelief. "Pearl, what are you talking about?"

It was then that Pearl realized what she had done. She quickly turned her back to Topaz so that she could not see the emotion rising in her face. Topaz grabbed her by the shoulders and spun her around.

"How do you know about Oscar, and when did you find out?"

Pearl mumbled, "It's complicated."

"These are not hard questions, Pearl. Could I please get an answer? Pearl, I asked you how you know about Oscar, and when did you find out?"

Pearl knew she was trapped. She did not want to lie to her trusting sister, and she knew there was no way to continue to deny her involvement with Oscar. Pearl tried very hard to soften the announcement.

"Oscar wants me to be his wife."

Topaz fell down in the chair. "Pearl, why would he want to marry you out of the blue?"

"It's not exactly out of the blue. For the last six months, we have grown close and developed a friendship."

Topaz was livid. "Pearl, you're insulting my intelligence. Grown close? It has to be a little deeper than that. Pearl, don't talk to me like I'm Ruby. Men don't propose to their buddies and make them first lady. Where did all this growing close take place? He's never been here, at least not in the evening with the family."

Pearl felt like she was ten years old in the principal's office. "He would spend time with me in the afternoons. Several times he went to the grocery store with me and helped me with my daily errands."

"Pearl, what was all the secrecy about?"

"It was just private and personal. I don't feel that we need to report our every move to each other."

"I don't mean how many times we go to the bathroom. I'm talking about important things like dating."

"We were not dating, we were—"

Topaz interrupted before she could finish the sentence, "I know, growing close. When Diamond was seeing Michael, she told us all about him. He had dinner with us several times, and she invited him to church for friends and family day. She was not sneaking around having secret rendezvous in the middle of the day."

"Now I'm insulted. You make me sound so dishonest. I didn't think it was even worth sharing. How can you even compare me to Diamond? She talks about everything. She doesn't even blow her nose unless we get a full description of how soft the tissue felt."

Topaz answered with tears forming in her eyes. "At least we don't have to find out key things that are going on in her life secondhand. You can take my plate away. I'm not hungry."

"But I made a beef stew. That is one of your favorites."

"I'm still full from the big lunch I had today. Maybe I'll eat some tomorrow." Topaz went upstairs and changed her clothes and sat on the back porch until it was time to go to bed.

Pearl cleared the table and set a plate for Ruby on the stove. Oscar called and told her he had seen Topaz at lunchtime. She told him he called too late because Topaz knew about his proposal. He told her that he was glad that she knew and stressed again how much he hated keeping their feelings a secret. He asked her if she wanted him to come over so that they could talk to Diamond, Topaz, and Ruby together. She told him that she was sure that Topaz would tell Diamond, and she would tell Ruby, but for right now she needed to be alone for a couple of days to help the family adjust to the news. He told her that he would give her two days, and then he would be over to talk with her in front of the family.

It was two in the morning when Pearl woke up to check the time. Her bed felt like a rock. She had tossed and turned all night and saw every hour on the clock. She finally gave up trying to sleep and decided to go downstairs to the kitchen to get some hot tea. After talking to Topaz, Diamond could not sleep. She went down to the kitchen a little after ten p.m., sat down in a chair, and had not moved since that time. When Pearl turned on the light in the kitchen, Diamond was sitting alone at the kitchen table. When Pearl faced Diamond, the look on her face was frightening; her eyes were as cold as ice.

"What's the matter, Pearl? Your conscience won't let you sleep?"

Pearl didn't know how to answer. She had never seen her sister look at her with such disdain.

After a moment she mumbled, "I just came to get some tea."

Diamond snapped back. "What you need to drink is truth serum."

Pearl turned to go back upstairs.

"Where are you going? You didn't get your tea."

"Diamond, I can't deal with you when you're being so sarcastic."

Diamond jumped off her chair as though she was on a spring.

"Sarcastic! You have the nerve to judge me when you've been carrying on an affair with Oscar Pelt for the past six months."

"Diamond, that is such an ugly word. I don't even know how to have an affair."

"Pearl, call it what you will if it makes you feel better, but you've been sneaking around like a thief in the night and lying. In my dictionary that spells affair." Pearl started back up the steps when Diamond spoke.

"Don't walk away from me, Pearl, this is not over."

Pearl attempted to climb the steps to escape upstairs. Diamond, close at her heels repeated, "Do not, do not walk away from this, Pearl. I remember a time when you preached to me that the family always comes first. You whipped me with guilt until I sacrificed all my dreams for the good of the family. You should have been listening to your own sermon. Why did Topaz have to hear about your marriage proposal by accident? Why were we all in the dark about your boyfriend? Do you hear me, Pearl?" Pearl, inwardly praying to end this confrontation in a futile effort to diffuse Diamond's anger, answered as calmly as she could, "Of course I hear you. Everybody in the neighborhood hears you, Diamond."

Diamond's rage, like a runaway train, could not be controlled. It was growing more intense with each sentence. She almost spat out her name.

"Pearl, big sister, dear, I'm waiting for you to give me one reason to trust and believe in you again, and I need that reason tonight." Pearl pushed past her and slumped into a kitchen chair. She put her head in her hands and began to cry. Diamond was unmoved. She walked to the counter and handed Pearl a napkin.

"I need answers, not tears. Topaz is disillusioned and disappointed because she thinks that you hung the moon. I'm angry. Forget angry, I am downright mad. It's not what you did. I'm glad to finally see that you're human like the rest of us. It's just how you did it. When is the wedding, or do we have to read about that in the paper too?"

"Diamond, I have not agreed to marry Oscar. There is no way I would make that kind of decision without discussing it with the two of you."

Diamond grunted and ignored Pearl. "Congratulations! Oscar Pelt is quite a catch."

"Are you listening to me at all? Nothing has been settled."

Diamond continued to talk as though Pearl was not even in the room and as if she was speaking to herself. "Don't be silly like I was, listening to you. Take this chance to have a life. Opportunities don't come knocking every day. Look at me. I'm teaching Michael Ramsey's daughter, a little girl that should be calling me Mother, not Miss Morgan. To add more insult to injury, I have to talk to him and his wife at parent-teacher conference every semester."

Pearl softened her tone. "Diamond, I wasn't trying to take anything away from you. I honestly thought when Mama and Daddy died that we should stay together for Ruby's sake as a family. Please believe that if nothing else."

Diamond looked at her with a blank expression. "Well, Pearl, you were wrong. Now you and Ruby can move to Arkansas and start a brand-new life while me and Topaz pick up the pieces of what's left of ours."

A HOUSE OF CARDS

After Diamond and Pearl's discussion in the kitchen, neither one slept. Diamond went upstairs to toss and turn
in her bed, and Pearl spent the remainder of the night on
the couch. When Pearl did awake after a restless slumber,
it was almost nine a.m. She was so grateful it was Saturday. On weekdays she always had to get Ruby up by seven
thirty a.m. so that she would not be late for school. She
was in eighth grade now, but she still would or could not
wake up on time independently. Nobody was up; she did
not hear any movement upstairs. She tiptoed up the stairs
to the bathroom. She peeked in Diamond and Topaz's
room. Their beds were empty. She did not hear them leave.
She was on the couch. If they had passed her, she would
have heard them close the front door; they must have gone
out the back. But where could they be this early in the
morning? Topaz worked on Saturdays, but her shift didn't
start until three p.m. She quietly opened Ruby's door. She
was sound asleep. She backed out slowly and tiptoed back

down the stairs to the kitchen and put on a pot of coffee. She called Evelyn's house, but there was no answer. She was about to hang up after the tenth ring when Joe answered with sleep in his voice telling her that Evelyn and Junior were at the clinic.

In a very annoyed tone he barked at her, "Evelyn told you she would be going this morning."

"I don't remember her telling me that."

"I was right in the room when she told you just a couple of days ago that Joe Jr. needed his shots for his school record." Before she could say anything, he slammed the phone down. Pearl was so preoccupied with her own problems that Joe's behavior did not faze her. She poured herself a cup of coffee and began to wipe the top of the refrigerator. It was already clean, but she needed to do something, anything, and for the time being, this was busy work.

Ruby came down the stairs wiping her eyes. "I was waiting for you to wake me up so we can get to the grocery store. If we don't hurry up, the lines will be so long and we'll never get out of there. I want to make chicken ala king for dinner tomorrow."

"You're really taking that cooking class to heart. I wish you would put that much effort in your history."

"Pearl, it's Saturday. Don't fuss. Since Diamond is the prize cook in this family, I just want to show her I can cook different stuff like she does. I'm going upstairs to get dressed and the list of things I need."

"You don't have to hurry. Diamond and Topaz are gone with the car."

"Gone where?"

"I don't know. They didn't leave a note."

Ruby was openly pouting. "Where are they this early? They know we always use the car on Saturday morning."

"I don't know where they are. I didn't even know they were gone until I looked in their room. Topaz has to be at work at three p.m., so they'll have to be back before then."

"The store will be so crowded by then."

"I know, Ruby, but there's nothing we can do about it." In an effort to cheer her up Pearl hugged her. "Let me fix a big country breakfast for the two of us. They aren't here, so we can eat their share. After we finish we can make a list of things we need at the store. Sit down. Let me put some grits on and bacon. I have a taste for some crispy bacon. Do you want eggs?"

Ruby was still disappointed. "Whatever you fix is all right with me."

Topaz and Diamond were at Daley's Diner having breakfast. The eggs, home fries, and biscuits they ordered were going untouched. Diamond was uncharacteristically picking at her eggs and moving them from side to side on her plate. Topaz pushed her food aside and made no pretense of eating. The coffee was cold, and the water glasses were still full. The waitress visited their table constantly.

"Is everything all right here? Can I bring you some warm coffee?"

Diamond answered without looking up. "We don't need any more coffee."

Ten minutes later she returned. "Excuse me, ladies, you haven't touched your food. Would you like something else?"

Diamond hissed. "We ordered what we wanted, and we know how to call you if we need anything."

Topaz was quiet and withdrawn, as she tended to be when she was hurt. Diamond was more vocal than usual, and several times the people in the diner turned to look at her as she spoke. Lowering her voice she talked through clenched teeth.

"What kills me about Pearl is the fact that she always hides behind the pretense that she didn't know she was doing anything wrong and never meant to hurt anybody. But all the time she's getting her way."

"I don't think she's dishonest. I just feel that her judgment is off," Topaz replied softly.

"Topaz, please, please don't defend her this morning. For the past six months she has been seeing Oscar and hiding it from everyone. You know that is dishonest."

"Dishonest or private?"

Diamond slammed her fork down at that remark. "You and I have been publicly supporting this family for years, and our lives are open books. Why should Pearl be the only one to have the luxury of privacy?"

"I thought about it all last night. Should we be this upset about Pearl finding a mate and happiness? Maybe she didn't tell us because she thought we would react just like we're doing. We're sisters, but we're separate people too. If Pearl goes to Arkansas with Oscar, it won't change our lives that much."

Diamond instantly defended her position. "You're missing the whole point. Pearl always makes major decisions about how we should live, but when it comes to her, we have no input."

"Is this the reason you're so upset, or are you a little bet resentful that it's Pearl instead of you?"

Diamond looked at Topaz as if she had cut her with a knife. "How can you say a thing like that to me? I don't resent Pearl. I love her."

"I know you love her, but face it, Diamond, everybody in the world knows that you're the pretty, outgoing, smart, well-dressed Morgan sister. You're so used to getting all the recognition and attention while Pearl was pushed in the background. It is very understandable that you feel that it should be you. I love you, Diamond, and I believe I know you better than anyone. In my heart I know that I'm right."

Diamond glared at her, grabbed her jacket, and stormed out of the restaurant. Topaz hurriedly paid the bill and ran behind her.

The next days there was an uneasy tension in the air in the Morgan household. Diamond and Topaz worked, Ruby went to school, and Pearl did her best to avoid Oscar. Two days later she was sweeping the front steps when Oscar drove up. He had tried to reach her by telephone all morning and was unsuccessful. This was the deadline date for his answer, and he was expectant and hopeful that Miss Pearl Morgan's name would soon change to Mrs. Pelt.

Pearl jumped when she saw his green Ford stop on a dime at the curb. He bounced out of the car and ran up the stairs. Pearl was so glad to see him. She was surprised how much she missed him in such a short time. He looked her straight in the eyes.

"Should I rent a tux or pack my bags? My whole future is in your lovely hands." Pearl smiled as he kissed her ring finger; she dropped the broom on the porch and led him inside. In the house he hugged her. "I wish you could stay in my arms all morning. I can't wait until we can tell everyone how we feel. I'm so happy, I want to take out a full page ad in the *Detroit Free Press*. "Oscar loves Pearl." Please take the handcuffs off my heart. Set if free. It only beats for you."

Pearl began by telling him how upset Diamond and Topaz were at her for keeping them in the dark. She was so sorry that she had caused a rift in the family. Oscar was sympathetic, but his main concern was her and their future.

"I do understand, Oscar, but my family is so important to me the thought that I hurt them hurts me more."

He tenderly held her face in his hands. "How can I make it better?"

"Tomorrow night come to dinner, and we will announce our plans for the marriage and the move, after that we will tell the church."

Oscar was beside himself with joy. "Did I hear you right? Our plans for marriage? You are going to really be my wife?"

"Yes, Oscar, and you will be my husband." For the first time in their entire courtship, Pearl kissed him first, long and passionate.

"Mrs. Pelt you curled my toes. Hallelujah!" He began to do the holy dance. "Let the church say amen!"

At dinner the next evening, the usual chatter and non-stop conversation was gone. Pearl set the table, and everyone took their seats as if it was the Spanish Inquisition. Diamond, Topaz, and Ruby sat on one side of the table, and Oscar and Pearl were seated across from them. Nobody commented on dinner, which surprised Pearl. She asked Evelyn to make her special corn pudding to go with the fried chicken, and she was sure that everyone would love it. Evelyn was in and out of Pearl's kitchen, trying to see what all the fuss was about dinner and why Oscar was invited, but Pearl's lips were sealed. She finally gave up and went home frustrated.

Oscar broke the silence. "I'm the luckiest man in Detroit tonight. I just had a meal fit for a king, and I'm surrounded by four beautiful women."

Ruby giggled. "I'm not a woman yet."

"No you're not grown, but you're a lovely young girl. I didn't grow up with sisters, so I always thought women talked all the time. Y'all so quiet I feel like a Baptist preacher in a Catholic church." Nobody laughed, so he got to the point of dinner. "Diamond, you and Topaz know that I have asked Pearl to marry me. The good news is that she has accepted."

Ruby was chewing and bit her tongue. "Pearl's going to get married?"

Oscar moved next to her and put his arms around her chair. "Yes, Ruby, we're all going to be one family."

Diamond started to leave the table when Oscar called after her. "Diamond, would you please stay?"

"I heard the news. Congratulations." She abruptly left the table. "I'm going upstairs. I have papers to grade for tomorrow."

"Everything is fine with me. I'm willing to help. I'll make Pearl's wedding dress if she wants me to, and we can start looking for patterns tomorrow."

Oscar spoke up quickly, "Could it wait just a few more minutes? I want to answer all questions and include everyone in the family in the decisions. You're a part of the wedding party, and we all appreciate and value your creativity."

Diamond did not stop moving. "Whatever you and Pearl decide is fine with me."

"Please sit back down. We have so much to cover and just a short time to do it that we all need to talk about it." Before she could answer, he had pulled out the chair for her and began to talk. "We're going to announce it in Sunday service. Because we have to be in Arkansas by the end of the month, things have to move quickly."

Ruby spoke up. "Pearl, you can't go to Arkansas. We need you here."

Pearl started to reply, but Oscar was too fast. "Don't worry, Ruby. You and Pearl are moving. We're all going to Arkansas."

Ruby turned her pleas to Pearl. "I don't want to live down south. In all the pictures I have seen about the South, everybody's got a rag on their heads and are picking cotton."

Pearl tried to comfort her. "Ruby, we'll live in a house. Oscar is going to be the minister, and we will never see cotton."

"I don't care. I don't want to move."

Oscar tried in vain to talk to her and explain to her the benefits of new surroundings, new friends, and new experiences. She refused to listen to him and left the table to go upstairs to her room.

Oscar was still optimistic. "She'll come around. She's just surprised, and we caught her off guard."

Topaz was more realistic. "I don't know, Oscar, she's a Morgan. The entire Morgan family is stubborn. She's lived here her whole life. This city is all she knows."

"But she'll have Pearl," Oscar protested.

"That's true, but Pearl is not her entire world. There are her friends at school and especially her dancing class. She loves dancing. She wants to be a dancer when she grows up."

Pearl voiced her disapproval, "I wouldn't encourage that. She can't make a living dancing. That's just a fantasy."

Diamond grunted. "Everybody needs a little fantasy, Pearl."

Oscar intervened. "Ladies, ladies, let's stay focused. Ruby is a little girl, and we are intelligent adults. Maybe the answer is letting Ruby finish the school year in Detroit and join us in the summer in Arkansas."

Diamond's eyes widened as she spoke in an elevated tone. "Leaving Ruby with us is not an option. Topaz and I have to work. Topaz works a swing shift, and she's on call for private duty if needed. I work two Saturdays a month at the Ford Center. We're both too busy to supervise Ruby. Pearl volunteered for that job a long time ago, and she can't drop it now when it's no longer convenient. It shouldn't be a problem. Pearl is a big fan of sacrifice. I'm glad you enjoyed dinner. I have to go upstairs and grade papers for tomorrow, so I'll say good night." Oscar started to rise from his seat.

"No don't get up. You're not a guest. You're family now."

Oscar, still positive, appealed to Topaz. "When I asked Pearl to marry me, she told me that Ruby would always be a part of our lives. If she can finish the school semester here, I think the adjustment would be smoother. As soon as school ends, we will come and get her and take her to her new home. It's important for Ruby's sake that the adults stay calm and not give in to her dramatics."

"Oscar, I understand what you're saying but Diamond is right. When Pearl leaves Detroit, Ruby will have to go with her. Right or wrong, Pearl is her mother, and we are her sisters. I'm going to say good night too. You and Pearl need to be alone so you can figure this out."

After she excused herself from the table, Oscar and Pearl sat together in silence. Pearl and Oscar's wonderful day was melting like a hot ice cream cone.

As the days went on, Pearl's attempts to convince Ruby to move to Arkansas were futile. She would not even listen to Pearl. Whenever Pearl opened the subject, Ruby ran to her room and threatened to run away from home if she was forced to leave Detroit.

Oscar was growing more and more impatient with Pearl's lack of discipline and was surprised that she would let a child dictate their future. They argued constantly, which always ended with Oscar scolding and Pearl crying. He wanted to know why Ruby was driving the bus and Pearl was just a passenger. Oscar's anger increased every time Pearl defended Ruby and did not fight harder for their life together. Finally she gave him no choice but to issue an ultimatum.

"Pack Ruby's things, act like an adult, and tell her she has no choice but to move or the wedding is off." The words were so difficult to say that he took the easy way out, called her, and told her on the telephone so he didn't have to look in her eyes and take it back. In reality he never wanted to cancel the wedding; he loved Pearl deeply, and he was willing to share parenting of Ruby. The ultimatum was meant to push Pearl into action. In the end, after much soul searching, Pearl did not love herself enough to fight for her happiness. She did not pack Ruby's things. Consequently, Oscar Pelt, with a heavy heart, went to Arkansas alone to accept his pastoral assignment.

DREAMS DEFERRED

After Oscar left, Pearl never spoke of him and would not discuss it with her sisters. This dream was locked away in her heart, and she never opened it again. She was so grateful that she and Oscar had never made the wedding announcement at church so that she did not have to endure the endless questions or condolences. She embraced this as a true sign that it was not meant to be.

That summer Ruby graduated from grammar school. She auditioned and was accepted into Cass Technical High School, which specialized in the performing arts. Their singing and dance programs were among the best in the Midwest. Pearl was disappointed when she was accepted; she had hoped that Ruby would have outgrown her fascination with dancing and would enroll in a more academic curriculum. She appealed to Diamond and Topaz for help to persuade Ruby to change her educational direction, but after Ruby's triumphant victory over Oscar, combined with years of excluding her sisters in Ruby's rearing, sadly

Pearl's lack of parental control finally reached the boiling point. As Ruby entered her teen years, she would listen to no one.

Topaz was also in school taking courses to teach. She had been promoted to head nurse on her floor and decided that the long hours and standing on her feet would eventually take its toll, so she opted for the next step. She completed her first semester with flying colors. The radiology course that she needed for her second semester was only offered in New York. It would mean staying there for five months. She was unsure that she could afford such a move, but the dean informed her that because she was a top student, the hospital would supply a stipend for her use, and she could stay in hospital-owned quarters if she agreed to teach in their facility for at least five years. All she had to do was sign a contract, and she would receive one hundred dollars a month for expenses.

Because she had never ventured outside of Detroit, she was dubious at first, but all her coworkers were so excited about the trip that she let herself get caught up in the adventure. Pearl was inquisitive about the trip, and Ruby wanted a picture of the Statue of Liberty. Diamond was quiet.

All of Diamond's life she had prayed to escape her humdrum existence, and now this gift was handed to Topaz, who didn't even want it on a silver platter. Topaz did her best to minimize the trip because she was sensitive to Diamond's feelings about never leaving Detroit. Although she tried very hard to ignore it, Ruby kept it on the front burner. The first thing in the morning at breakfast and the last thing at night at dinner, Ruby went on and on about the Big Apple. Topaz tried to change the subject, but she would continue her quest for information about the city. Diamond was mostly silent during these meals and excused herself a couple of nights before dinner was over. Jones Tabernacle raised a special collection for her trip and gave her a farewell party. When Topaz was packing for the trip, Diamond made sure she was not home. She purposely worked late so that she was not available to take her to the train station. Pearl drove her, and Ruby and Evelyn tearfully kissed her goodbye. On the way home, Pearl reflected on the fact that Topaz was the one that everybody least expected to be the first to leave home.

When the train pulled out of the station Topaz was panic stricken for a moment. This was really happening; she was leaving. She calmed herself and looked out of the window as the train left the station and memorized Ruby's excited expression and Pearl's concern. The last picture she had of them was Ruby waving frantically and Pearl blowing a kiss. She wished with all her heart that Diamond had been able to find the courage to come. She understood her envy and did not fault her. She already missed her most of all. She made a vow that she would find away to persuade her to come to New York to visit her as soon as possible.

The morning that Topaz left, Diamond did everything in her power to stop thinking about the trip. She went to school early to change her bulletin boards—a task she knew would occupy her mind and thoughts. She hated herself for not being able to go to the station with Topaz, but as hard as she tried, she could not face her leaving for

New York while she stayed in Detroit. She had stopped questioning God years ago about the unfairness of her life and had come to accept the sameness, but this was an unexpected blow that she had not counted on.

"Topaz going to New York." It was even hard for her to say the words *New York, Broadway, Macy's, Times Square, the biggest city in the United States.* That was the kind of break that dreams were made of. Topaz had never even talked about traveling, and it had been Diamond's obsession from childhood. Topaz had stepped into her dream and was living it.

When Pearl, Evelyn, and Ruby left the train station, Ruby was too excited to go to school. Evelyn was talking non-stop about how lucky Topaz was and how she could not wait to get her first postcard from New York City. Because they were so keyed up, Pearl suggested that Ruby skip school and they spend the rest of the morning window-shopping and have lunch at Woolworth's.

While they were shopping, Ruby wandered off. When Pearl caught up with her, she asked her what she was looking for.

"I want to get a present for Diamond."

Pearl was shocked. "It's not her birthday. Is there something special going on I don't know about?"

"No, but she's been so sad since Topaz left. I want to cheer her up. When she's not happy, it's no fun at home."

Pearl was pleased, Ruby usually only thought about herself. "I'm proud of you Ruby. You're growing up. That is so sweet and caring. Buy whatever you want."

Ruby chose a lovely purple scarf that just screamed Diamond and had it gift wrapped. Pearl thought the scarf was a little pricey and the gift-wrapping excessive, but she bought it anyway. She saw it as an investment in the development of Ruby's character.

When Ruby set the table for dinner that evening, she put Diamond's present beside her plate. Diamond tore into the package like Christmas morning.

"Oh my goodness! What a lovely scarf. Pearl, did you buy this?"

"No, Ruby got it for you."

"Ruby, how sweet and so classy. I don't have anything nice enough to wear this with. I'll have to make a new dress."

Ruby was so pleased. "Do you really like it, or are you just saying it not to hurt my feelings? It's so hard to pick anything out for you because you always wear the right thing."

"I love it, but what did I do to deserve it?"

"You're pretty, and you should have pretty things."

Pearl shook her head as she cleared the table. Another Diamond all over again. As much as she had wanted Ruby to follow in her path, as she matured she was turning into a younger version of Diamond, all charm and charisma.

As soon as Topaz got settled, she called Diamond. They talked for over an hour.

"Hello? Is this the Morgan residence? I'm looking for the one named Diamond. Is she home?"

"That depends on who wants her." Diamond had a smile in her voice, and Topaz was glad to hear her happy again.

"I missed you at the station."

"I'm sorry, but it was just too hard—," Topaz stopped her in mid-sentence and changed the subject.

"Don't get buried in the bedroom while I'm gone. You never hang up anything or put anything back. The room is going to be a mess. I don't know what you will do without me to clean up after you."

"I'm going to surprise you when you get back. The bedroom will look like the cover of *House Beautiful*."

"I have a better surprise. All the way up here I was thinking that we could plan a weekend together."

Diamond screamed so loud Topaz dropped the phone.

"I should have written you. I hope my hearing isn't damaged."

Diamond was in a world of her own. "Do you mean it? Don't tease me. I can hardly wait. Me in New York! Next stop, Broadway. I won't tell anybody until I have my ticket. I don't want to jinx it."

Topaz laughed. "This is a sure thing. Good night Broadway, baby."

For the first time in two weeks Diamond went to bed and slept peacefully.

Topaz was having a hard time adjusting to a school routine. It had been years since she was a student, and the rhythm of balancing classes and studying were not as easy as she remembered. When she first got to New York, she promised Ruby she would send her a souvenir weekly, but her class load left her with so little energy that after school she either went to the library or fell into bed. Her classmates were all younger than she was, and they teased her mercilessly saying, "All work and no play makes Jane a dull nurse." Never one to be a joiner, the taunts rolled off her back like water on a duck. She was certain that once she acclimated and developed a plan that she could have somewhat of a social life. Her idea to organize her class work and try to work in some time to invite Diamond to come and visit her was getting further and further away from her. The classes were very intense, and she found herself studying most nights and weekends.

Diamond was at home living on Topaz's promise that she would invite her to New York. She was secretly buying clothes and shoes so that she would look big city and not like a country hick. New shoes always made her walk just a little differently, and new clothes make her stand up straighter. Ruby had all the postcards that Topaz sent her on the fridge and on the mirror in her bedroom. Every time Diamond would pass the fridge, she would rub one of the postcards for good luck.

Topaz was having such difficulties at school that her grades were slipping. She constantly studied and joined study groups, but nothing seemed to help. A note in her mailbox told her to report to the Dean of Studies. She read it twice, then folded it up and buried it in her purse. All the way to the office, she tried in vain to stay calm. When she faced the dean, his demeanor confirmed her fears.

"Good afternoon, Miss Morgan. I've been reviewing your test scores. Given the fact that you're not a student nurse, and that you have years of experience, they are dis-appointing. The terms of a scholarship program require the student to maintain a B average."

"Dean Coppin, believe me, I don't take this opportu-nity lightly. I'm very serious."

"Miss Morgan, I can see you have good intentions, but rules tie my hands. This often happen to students from smaller cities. In larger schools the competition is intense, and some students get lost in the pool. I called you in today as a warning. This is not a dismissal yet."

Topaz was crestfallen; she had never failed in the past. True, she always had to study, but she always managed to move from class to class. Painful as it was, she had to admit to herself that she would have to leave the program. What distressed her the most was the disappointment her family would feel if she didn't complete this program. Pearl would understand. Ruby was so excited and was bragging about her to everyone, and she did not want her to be embar-rassed in front of her friends. Diamond was holding her breath waiting for Topaz's call; she even considered get-ting her hair cut when she saw a bob style in a magazine but at the last minute got cold feet and changed her mind. Every night she sat by the phone in anticipation. The call never came. The week she made up her mind to call New York, when she picked up the phone to dial the number, Topaz was on the other end trying to call her at the same time. She was so sure that she had willed the call and was so excited at the prospect of going to New York that she missed the disappointed tone in Topaz's voice.

"Topaz, can you believe this? How many times does this happen? I thought you had forgotten our phone number. Tell me everything about the Big Apple. Have you eaten at the Automat yet?"

"No, Diamond. I don't have time to leave school. The classes have been too hard."

"It's just because you haven't been to school in a long time. It'll just take a little time to find your rhythm. You know what Daddy always said, 'We Morgans are like cream. We always rise to the top.'"

"Not this time, Diamond. My scores and grades were not high enough, so I have been dropped from the program. I'm coming home next week."

Diamond held the phone, fighting back tears. Her concern for her sister's feelings overrode her own disappointment. "So what? You have a job here that you love, and they love you. How many times are you going to get a free trip to New York? It's their loss. When you get back, we'll do something special. Put this behind you, okay?"

They both lightly put the phone in the receiver. Topaz whispered to the mute phone, "Okay, Diamond. Love you."

After the call Diamond went to bed determined that she was going to spend some time away from Detroit. The next day she went to the office and applied for two weeks' vacation so that she and Topaz could go across the river and spend a week in Canada.

Diamond was rejuvenated with a new burst of energy making plans for their trip. She pored over brochures and planned a tour of the most famous sites. She found a small inn that was reasonably priced, and she booked a room with a view of the northern lights.

"Pearl, I'm taking the car next week for our vacation."

"Diamond, how are we going to live a whole week without transportation? You and Topaz don't need it. You'll be relaxing all week with room service and tour buses while I have my daily errands here. Ruby has her piano and dance lessons. I have choir practice and the grocery store. I need the car."

"Pearl, we don't have enough money to take the train. The car is ours, not yours. I don't need your permission to use it."

"Diamond, why do you feel the need to turn every conversation into a disagreement? Take the car. I'll ask different people at church to drive us back and forth, or maybe Ruby can go with you and Topaz. She can stay in the same room. She's not a baby. she won't be any trouble. Travel is so educational. It would be memorable for her."

Diamond cleared her throat. "Pearl, everything does not revolve around Ruby. I planned this trip to cheer Topaz up after New York, and it's my first real vacation. I'm surrounded by children all day long at work, and next week I'm only going to spend my time with adults."

"Topaz needs this diversion to make her feel better about being dropped from the program, and I need this trip to keep breathing."

When Pearl saw the determination in Diamond's face she relented. "I will get Sister Conley and Sister Harris to help me with transportation while you're gone."

MOVING ON

When Topaz got home from New York, she barely had time to unpack before it was time to pack again to go on her holiday to Windsor, Canada. Diamond was so animated she was almost walking on air. They stayed up late every night planning and plotting their adventure.

Pearl and Ruby felt like they were on the outside looking in. For an entire week, Diamond and Topaz only spoke to each other. Every other evening they were downtown shopping for vacation items. Fearing that they might run out of her money, at the last minute Diamond went to the teacher's credit union and withdrew two hundred dollars.

Pearl shook her head.

"Diamond, I don't mean to overstep, but I feel I must say something. You're spending too much money. I know you want to have a good time, but buying new clothes and shoes for a week is not necessary. Your closet is full of clothes, and you have enough shoes for three people. You work too hard for your money to waste it. Pulling down money from your savings is foolish. That should be used for rainy day emergencies."

Diamond, determined not to let her spoil her joy, nonchalantly answered, "It's none of your affair, Pearl. I make the money, and I'll spend it any way I want to. You're not only stepping in my business, you're jumping all over it. It's raining in my life. In fact, I feel like I'm in the middle of my monsoon season."

Two days before their departure, Diamond and Topaz's language had almost turned into secret, giddy schoolgirl code. The day they left Pearl had insisted that Reverend Barnes come over to pray for a safe trip. Before they pulled out of the driveway, maps in hand, Reverend Barnes placed his hand on the car and blessed the trip. As soon as the last "amen" was uttered, Diamond put her pedal to the metal, and they started on their journey. Ruby, Pearl, and Reverend Barnes had to literally jump out of the way and were eating fumes as the car sped down the street.

The drive from Detroit to Canada was leisurely and pleasant. The initial plan was to split the hour commute in half. Diamond would take the first half hour and Topaz the last shift.

It was October, and the scenery was postcard beautiful. The trees were almost completely changed. The shades of gold, orange, and purple leaves were breathtaking. Diamond had planned to sleep as Topaz drove, but she didn't want to miss anything. Her nose was pressed against the car window just like a kid in a candy store. Twice she asked Topaz to stop the car so that she could take pictures of the trees.

It was approaching noon when they reached the inn. Diamond had purposely hidden the brochure from Topaz so that she didn't know what to expect. In the shadows it resembled a medieval castle. The Camelot Inn was a magnificent fortress of buildings that looked like a picture in a fifteenth-century history book. The buildings were all white, and the windows were stained glass. The sun glowing through the windows reflected a prism of kaleidoscope colors. As Topaz drove closer to the inn, she abruptly stopped the car. Diamond, drowsy by now, was afraid they were having car trouble.

"What's wrong?"

Topaz turned to her, misty eyed, and answered, "Nothing's wrong. I just feel like Cinderella, and I need a minute to believe that I'm not dreaming."

Diamond playfully pinched her. "Come on, Cindy. Let's drive up to the door before you turn into rags."

The inn had more than adequate parking space for its small number of registered guests. When they walked up to the entrance, the front doors automatically opened. The lobby was small but quietly elegant. The couch and the chairs were larger and over-stuffed, homey, and comfortable. Two impressive shelves were filled to overflowing with hardcover books. A sign on the bookshelves boasted that many of them were first editions. The front desk was oval-shaped mahogany wood that was polished to a mirror-like finish.

They were so mesmerized by the surroundings that neither one of them heard the front desk clerk manager as he asked them to register. When he asked the third time in an elevated voice, Diamond snapped to attention. He immediately apologized and spoke in a much softer tone.

To avoid asking the obvious question, she moved away from the desk and began to subconsciously read the tourist guidebooks on the coffee tables.

"Excuse me, miss. I need your name." When she finally came down to earth and gave her name, she really looked at the desk clerk. Their eyes met for just a moment, and a bolt of electricity passed through them that temporarily made it impossible for either of them to move.

When the bellhop came to take the suitcases to their room Jon waved him away and picked up both bags and led them to the elevator. The elevator was a manual one with a metal gate that he pulled shut and turned the wheel to their floor. They were on the third floor, room 306. Jon was very glad that their room was so close to the elevator because the suitcases were heavy. *Perhaps I was too hasty in picking these up*, he thought to himself. He was tired and did not want these two ladies to see him winded. He was glad to drop them to open the door to their room. It was the prettiest room they had ever seen. It looked like the cover of *House Beautiful*. The room had two full-size canopy beds with peach ruffled bed coverings and canopy covers to match. The window overlooking the tree-lined garden had matching curtains. Jon was pleased that they approved and went on to explain the extras at the inn.

On Friday nights they had a three-piece combo that played live music in the lounge. Every morning they served free continental breakfast and a free newspaper. As soon as Jon was gone and they were sure he was out of ear range, they fell on the beds and giggled like teenagers. They were tired but too excited to sleep. They took turns taking showers. The water was so relaxing, it was finally clear to both of them that they needed a nap until dinner. Topaz, fearing they might sleep through the night, called the front desk and asked for a seven p.m. wake up call. When they woke up, they were refreshed and ready for their first evening in Canada. Dressed in their new casual "vacation clothes," pedal pushers with matching jackets, they looked like ladies of leisure. Never content to not stand out in a crowd, Diamond slipped on her new gold pumps to add a touch of glamour. With a last look of approval in the mirror, they strolled to the elevator.

While in the lobby, they went to the front desk for suggestions on where to eat dinner. The desk was unattended. They rang the bell once but were too impatient to wait and left. It was already well after eight p.m., and they were hungry. As they turned the corner in the parking lot, they bumped into Jon.

He smiled. "You girls have got to stop following me. Are you off to see the town?"

"Not right now. Diamond and I are looking for a nice place to eat."

"What do you have a taste for?"

"I just want food. Diamond, do you want anything special?"

Diamond was uncharacteristically compliant. "It doesn't matter."

"In that case ladies, you're in luck. I'm off duty, and I'll take you to one of our most popular restaurants. If I'm not intruding, I'd love to join you for dinner."

Topaz hesitated, but Diamond's enthusiastic "yes" was an unmistakable welcome. She answered quickly for two reasons: one, she did not want to spend time searching for a restaurant, and two, because she really wanted to spend more time with Jon. The electricity she first felt when she met him at the inn was multiplied by a thousand. Chills were literally racing through her entire body. Standing next to him her defenses were melting like butter on hot toast.

In the parking lot he was dressed in gray slacks and a silky gray shirt to match. He was average height; she only had to look up slightly to meet his coal-black eyes, which were the exact color of his shiny curly hair. It was hard to pinpoint his ethnicity. He was neither Negro nor White, but a mixture of two races that she could not readily identify.

He stopped them from going to their car but instead led them both to his, a brand-new spit-polish clean Buick. Diamond could not help thinking how extravagant it was for a desk clerk. It was midnight blue with light blue interior; the car was so clean she could eat off the floor. Topaz instinctively opened the back door so that Diamond could sit in the front seat. When Diamond settled in next to him, he patted her hand. Jon drove them six blocks down to a lovely restaurant that looked much too expensive for them, but he assured him that it was affordable. When he stopped the car, he opened the doors for Topaz and Diamond. Topaz thanked him; Diamond smiled. He returned her smile with a wink. The crescent moon shone brightly, and the sky was a blanket of twinkling stars. The neon sign on the restaurant spelled out, "The Retreat, Where the Elite Meet and Greet." Diamond silently thanked God that she was wearing her pretty gold shoes.

When they stepped into the foyer of the restaurant, they were immediately greeted by a French hostess. At first they were at a loss as how to handle this when Jon spoke to the hostess in perfect French with such sophistication that they dropped their jaws, impressed and then delighted. This desk clerk was becoming more and more interesting every minute. The restaurant was busy yet intimate at the same time. They were seated at a table near the window so they could see the passing parade of people coming and going. The lighting was dim, with a candle on each table. Diamond wanted to take a picture and almost took her Brownie from her camera bag but decided not to when Topaz whispered that it would make them look like not-used-to-nothing hicks. Diamond had a standing rule that whenever she was eating out, she always ordered something she had never tasted. She chose lamb chops with mint jelly for no other reason than it sounded exotic. Jon told the waiter he would have the same. Topaz, less adventurous, ordered perch, but Diamond made her change.

"We're on vacation. Splurge."

Topaz changed her order to steak. They had strawberry shortcake for dessert. Dinner was delicious. It tasted even better because they did not have to cook it or wash the dishes. Topaz was a little dubious when the waiter left the bill. She insisted they pay for their dinner.

Topaz whispered to Diamond, "We can't let him spend this kind of money on us. He's just trying to impress us—I mean you. The man is a desk clerk. He's probably spending his whole week's salary tonight."

"I'll handle this, ladies."

"Give it to me, Jon. Topaz and I are fully prepared to pay for our dinner."

"No way. I consider myself a gentleman. I couldn't sleep tonight if I let two ladies I had dinner with pay the bill."

"Diamond, come to the ladies' room with me."

Diamond, checking her hair in the mirror and bored with Topaz's seriousness, nonchalantly added, "He has a beautiful car."

"I would bet the rent he doesn't own that expensive car. He probably borrowed it for the evening."

"He's been flirting with you from the moment he saw you, and he just wants to show off for you. If he spends this money tonight, he will probably be broke all week. When we get back to the table, I will tell him that we will pay our own bill."

When they returned to the table the waiter told them that Jon left a message that he would meet them in the parking lot when they returned from the ladies' room. Topaz tried to give the waiter a tip, but he told her that the gentleman had covered the bill and tip before he left.

Topaz said, "We must find a way to pay him back. It would only be right."

Diamond did not agree. "It would only embarrass him. When you do something nice for someone, you're doing it because you want to and not looking for payback in return. We should not even mention it. We have both spent too much time in Sunday school not to recognize and appreciate manna from heaven."

Topaz frowned. Diamond giggled. "Relax, it's just a joke. Trust me, you won't go to hell for laughing."

Jon was standing by his car, waiting for them smoking a cigarette; the blue smoke circled around his head and formed a halo. He offered both of them one, but they refused.

He held the cigarette between his teeth as he spoke, "That's all right. I smoke enough for the three of us." The ride to the inn was short and silent. Topaz in the back seat looked out at the beautiful calm night and reflected on the difference between this serene evening and the noisy car horns and traffic lights in the busy streets of Detroit. Diamond's thoughts were far removed from home; her mind was in the front seat of the car. She was not looking back or thinking about tomorrow. She was completely engulfed in this moment. Jon looked over and pressed a coin in her hand. She looked at the penny, puzzled. He broke out in laughter.

"I'm paying you for a glimpse into your deep thoughts."

Diamond's voice dripped with honey as she held out a turned up hand. "A penny is too cheap for my thoughts. You owe me at the very least a quarter." When they returned to the room, Topaz fell on the bed.

"I'm tired and stuffed. All I want to do right now is sleep. Taking off my clothes seems like too much work."

Diamond wanted to talk to her about the evening, but as soon as Topaz's head touched the pillow she fell into a deep slumber. The entire night Diamond hardly closed her eyes. She fantasized about Jon until the wee hours of the morning, and when she drifted off to sleep she dreamed about him the rest of the night.

Diamond was not alone in her insomnia. Jon paced the floor all night thinking about her. He wanted to go up to her room and bring her to his house. It was like he had been suspended in time waiting for her to walk into his life. He could not get over the fact that these two ladies drove all by themselves from Detroit. That kind of independence was so exciting. Topaz was unpretentious and classy, but Diamond was special. She was not only beautiful to look at but blessed with the kind of sex appeal that drove men crazy. It impressed him that all evening they both downplayed their professional jobs because they didn't want to make him feel inferior; therefore, he didn't have a chance to tell them that he was one-third owner of the inn. He was filling in at the front desk the day they arrived because two employees were out sick. He had been steadily dating Denise Kidd for well over a year. She was a file clerk with the Canadian Tourist Agency. Before he met Diamond Morgan, he was sure that Denise was the woman he would marry.

The next four days of the vacation, Topaz saw Canada. She went on tourist buses and visited museums alone. She brought souvenirs to take home and sent postcards home and signed Diamond's name. While Topaz was seeing Canada, Diamond was seeing Jon. After he told Diamond he was part owner of the inn, all her inhibitions about a relationship vanished. Topaz cautioned her about the danger of a broken heart that accompanied a vacation romance, but Diamond shut her out. She could not think beyond this day. She lost the man she loved once, and this time she vowed it was not going to happen again. As usual she chose to jump heart first in the deep end of the pool.

Jon romanced, wined, and dined her, and they spent every waking minute together. She moved out of her room at the inn into his house. He made love to her as though he had invented it, mind, body, and soul. For the first time in her life, Diamond felt complete. Jon ignited her dormant fires and the blaze made her glow from head to toe. It was unadulterated passion, given and returned with equal intensity. He served her breakfast in bed every morning and massaged her feet at night. He taught her how to smoke; brought her a gold lighter with engraved initials D and J, and soon they were sharing cigarettes. They talked late into the night about their childhoods and discovered they had both experienced great losses at an early age. She told him about the death of her parents and how for years she cried every Tuesday, the day she found out about the accident and how dramatically it changed the course of her life.

He was an illegitimate war child, born to an Italian mother and a Negro soldier during World War II. His father deserted them when he was discharged. His mother, unable to support him and ostracized by her family, abandoned him, and he was adopted by a Canadian couple when he was six years old. He grew up with the hurt of never knowing his real father. When he was a boy, every Father's Day was painful for him. It was a story that he swore he had never shared with anyone but her. To secure his time with Diamond, he told Denise that he was working on an audit for the inn and for at least a week he would not be available. He pulled Diamond close and kissed her passionately.

"Please stay here with me. I can't stand to see you go. I never believed in love at first sight before, but I couldn't love you more if I had known you my whole life." He kissed her again, so long and hard, she had to pull away to get her breath.

Tearfully, she begged, "Come to Detroit with me. I didn't know how empty my life was until you touched me. Love at first is rare, but it's real. My father always told us how he knew the minute he met my mother that she would be his wife. They met in Belle Isle, a park in Detroit. She was walking with her sisters, and he said his heart literally skipped a beat when he saw her. He asked her three times to marry him before she said yes. Through good and bad times and four children, they loved each other until the day they left this world together. Growing up I thought they had such a beautiful love story, and I always dreamed about meeting my one true love."

He kissed her eyes, her tearstained cheeks, and finally her waiting lips. After the kiss, she rested her head on his shoulder. "Was your mother as pretty as you?"

"*Stunning* was the word Daddy used. Her hair was bright red, and he said when she stood in sunlight, it looked like her whole head was on fire. He loved her hair. He couldn't keep his hands out of it.

Stroking her hair, he pledged his heart to her. "Angel you don't have to dream about love anymore. I am yours, mind, soul, and body."

Neither one of them could see the future without each other.

TRUTH

Topaz and Diamond's holiday was fast coming to an end. Jon and Diamond still had not settled their living arrangements. For the time being, Diamond said that she would be back during Christmas break from school. It was three long months away and not enough, but at least it was something to look forward to. On Diamond and Jon's last night together, he gave her a silver necklace with two intertwined hearts. She promised she would wear it forever.

Diamond was at the inn helping Topaz pack on their last day in Canada. Jon made sure he was not around. Topaz wondered where he was, and Diamond's quick answer was he probably could not bear to see her leave and purposely stayed away. It seemed strange to Topaz that Jon was not there to say goodbye, but Diamond said she understood perfectly; he could not bear to see her go. Topaz did not agree, but Diamond was so sure she was right, she did not argue with her.

"As soon as I get home I will call him, and between now and Christmas we will have long romantic telephone calls and letters, and then I will be back in his arms at Christmas. Merry Christmas to me." She began to hum "White Christmas."

Topaz cautioned, "Diamond, Christmas is a long time away."

Diamond's confident answer convinced Topaz. "The old cliché about absence makes the heart grow fonder—Jon and I will make it reality." Jon rushed into the room.

"I'm so glad I caught you. Diamond, I need to talk to you."

"What is it? You look like you've been running."

"I just didn't want to miss you."

Topaz, feeling like a third wheel, offered to take a bag to the car. Out of breath, Jon said, "I want you to stay the rest of the day. Diamond and I have some unfinished business we need to take care of right now."

Topaz was confused. "Another day? We've already checked out. I'm sure this room is booked for someone else."

Jon laughed. "I'm innkeeper here. I can make any adjustments as needed." Diamond's mind was racing. *Business? Maybe he's going to buy me a ring.*

Topaz again said, "Diamond, I'll start putting some bags in the trunk."

Diamond stopped her. "You don't have to leave. Jon's, what's so important that we can't leave today?"

"Diamond, you believe I love you, and my life started the minute I looked in your eyes."

"What's the matter? What are trying to say?"

"Do you believe I love you?"

"Yes, Jon, I believe you."

"There's no pretty way to say this, so I have to just say it. I live with a woman. We've talked about getting married next year."

For a painful second the only sound in the room was Topaz. "My God. Where has she been this week while you were wining and dining my sister?"

"I told her I was doing an audit for the inn and would be tied up for the week."

"Diamond, let's just go home."

"Please don't leave until you to hear me out. I don't want to be with her another minute. She was my past. I want a future with you. I want to show you I mean every word I'm saying. I was on the way to tell her it's over, but I want to take you with me. I don't ever want to hide anything from you ever again."

Topaz hugged her sister. "Diamond, this isn't right. You can't do this. Can you still trust this man?"

"Topaz I love your sister. I promise you I will not hurt her."

Diamond pulled away from Topaz. "Diamond please..."

"I hear you, but I have to follow my heart." She took Jon's hand. "I'll go with you. I have to see this all the way to the end. I can't just walk away."

"Be careful. I'll be here when you get back."

"I know, Topaz. I know."

Diamond and Jon arrived at the house, Diamond clutched his hand tightly. When they reached the door, Denise, Jon's girlfriend opened it.

"Welcome home. You didn't tell me you were bringing company home."

Jon was non-responsive. "Can we just get out of the doorway and move into the house?"

When Diamond entered the house she sat in the first chair she saw. Jon sat on one end of the couch and Denise on the other. Diamond was surprised how attractive she was, she was tall and slender with a short curly bob. She and Jon made a handsome couple. The house smelled like home cooking.

"Denise this is Diamond Morgan."

"Diamond, that's an unusual name. Who is she? Why is she here in our home, Jon?"

"We met last week at the inn, she and her sister were on vacation."

"What's her sister's name? Sapphire?"

"We spent a lot of time together, and we're in love. They live in Detroit, and I will be spending a lot of time there. I'm going to be moving out." Denise jumped off the couch.

"One week? You have the nerve to tell me you love her after we have a year together!"

She stood in front of Diamond, glaring. "Do you talk? Or is your specialty stealing engaged men?"

Diamond rose to face her. "I didn't steal him."

Jon stepped between them. "Denise, this is so ugly and I'm so sorry. I didn't plan this. It just happened."

"This tender love story may not have the happy ending you are hoping for."

Diamond tugged at Jon's sleeve. "Let's go. I want some air."

"Not yet, honey. While he was busy with you, I went to the doctor."

Jon's concern was evident. "Are you sick?"

"I'm not sick, but I found out yesterday that you're going to be a father in eight months."

Jon stammered in disbelief. "The doctor is sure?"

Denise was victorious because she knew she held the trump card. "As sure as sure can be."

Diamond's legs gave way and she collapsed into the chair. "This can't be happening. It's a bad dream or a soap opera. It can't be real." Rising from the chair, she paced as she talked. "A baby! Why didn't she tell you before today? This is the perfect time to bring it up." Until that revelation she had been content to let Jon speak for them, but now she knew she was in a fight, one she was determined to win.

Denise shot back, "Not that it's any of your business, but I just found out yesterday! Jon get her out of here, we need to talk about our baby."

Diamond screamed, "Get used to it! I'm not going anywhere!"

Jon, fighting to get control, spoke as calmly as he could, "Diamond and I are leaving. I have to get her back to the inn. I'll be back later."

When they got in the car, Diamond collapsed in tears. Jon did his best to console her. "Don't cry. It tears me apart to see you this way. I know this is bad, but it's not hopeless."

"Jon if it's your baby, you're stuck with her."

"It is. I'm sure of that, but I'm not stuck. I will work things out with Denise."

His answer left her confused. "Work out? What does that mean?"

"Darling, you know I can't walk away from my child. I have to support her during the pregnancy and flesh out the details of sharing custody."

"It gets worse and worse. That means you can't leave Canada."

"Yes I can. I need more time. Just give me a month"

"A month? That long?"

"We weren't going to be together until Christmas anyway, so plans haven't really changed. I'll call you every day, and next month I'll be on your doorstep. Nothing will ever come between us." He kissed her, and she melted in his arms.

While Diamond and Topaz were vacationing in Canada, Pearl was at home planning Ruby's sweet sixteen party. On December eighteenth Ruby would be sixteen, and Pearl promised her a party she and Detroit would never forget. She was making preparations to rent the Warwick Ball-room when Topaz and Diamond returned home. Pearl was shocked when Diamond lit a cigarette. Topaz ignored it and waved the smoke away, but Ruby thought it was cosmopolitan. Diamond proudly talked nonstop about Jon. Every conversation was centered on her future husband. They had never seen her so happy. Topaz supplied all the news about Canada.

When Pearl told Diamond and Topaz she was pulling out all the stops for the sweet sixteen party, she got no resistance from Diamond, which was a first. The whole church was invited, as well as the students in Ruby's dance class and her entire junior class. The party was to be catered, which angered Evelyn who swore no caterer could outdo her in the kitchen. She was also hurt because she considered herself a part of the family and wanted to be included in the party. To soothe her feelings, Pearl let her be in charge of the decorations, the color scheme was peach and tan. A local dance band was hired to supply the music, and a professional photographer was hired because she wanted the pictures developed in sepia print.

Pearl wanted to take her shopping for her dress, but Ruby insisted that she wanted Diamond to make it for her. She felt Pearl's taste was too plain, and she knew that Diamond would make her a one-of-a-kind creation. She and Diamond began shopping for the material and the pattern. Pearl wanted her to have a white dress, but Ruby had other ideas. She did not want to look like a little girl, and she was sure that if she left it up to Pearl, that's exactly what would happen. She and Diamond found a pattern that was pretty but mature at the same time. It was strapless, but the bodice was covered with diaphone netting. The skirt was not formfitting but slightly A-line, which outlined the body shape. Diamond thought the dress was too grown up for a sixteen-year-old party, but Ruby begged her to buy the pattern until finally she wore her down. Ruby wanted the dress to be red. Diamond put her foot down and refused; red was too risqué. Diamond compromised on a copper penny crepe satin that complimented Ruby's skin tone perfectly. Ruby was sure that no one else would have a dress that color, so she was satisfied. Pearl's birthday present for Ruby was their mother's pearls. When she asked Diamond and Topaz what they planned to give her, they unanimously said, "The party is our present."

Diamond had been home for two weeks, and she had not heard from Jon. When she called him at home, she was told he was at the inn. When she called the inn, he was never available. None of her messages were ever returned. At first she reasoned that he was busy trying to catch up on the work he missed because he spent so much time with her when she was there. When the logic stopped working, she began to get scared. She kept a good face in front of the family, but inside she was shaking like jelly. She was glad that all the activity and focus in the house was geared toward the party.

Pearl asked her to invite Jon. It would be a perfect time to introduce him to all their friends. He could sit at the family table. Diamond thought it would be a great time to show him off, but secretly she did not know if she could reach him in time. She mailed him an invitation with a personal note saying how much the family wanted to meet him and how much she needed an escort for the evening. She signed the note, "Yours, love and kisses."

ACCEPTANCE

The party was a huge success. It was the talk of the church for months after it was over. Everybody agreed that Ruby was gorgeous. Pearl gave her the pearl necklace and a corsage that contained sixteen tiny sugar cubes. When Pearl placed the pearls around her neck, she couldn't help but reflect on all the years prior to this day. Her decision to leave school and shoulder the responsibility of becoming head of her family had not been in vain. There had been ups, downs, and sacrifices throughout the years, but Ruby had turned into a lovely, well-educated, cultured young woman. Looking at Ruby, she was fulfilled and hoped her parents would be proud. Everybody said that Diamond outdid herself with Ruby's dress, and she was flooded with prom dress orders. Looking closely at the family pictures that were taken that night, Diamond's luscious red mouth was smiling, but her eyes were dead.

A week after the party, Diamond was lying in bed, going through her weekly mail and found a letter from

Jon. She had thought about him every second of every hour of every day since the last time she saw him. Her fingers shook as she tore open the envelope. She sat up in bed and read the letter.

My Dearest Darling,

I'm sorry I waited so long to contact you. I married Denise. She threatened that if I didn't make the baby legitimate, she would never let me be a part of its life. Maybe she was lying, but I couldn't take that chance. As much as I love you, I can't walk away from my blood. I know I promised I would never hurt you. The words "I'm sorry" seems so inadequate, but I'm deeply sorry for you and me. I hope one day you can forgive me. I will always love you.

Jon.

I married Denise. She read that until her tears turned the words into a blur. Her heart was broken. Eternal love for her would always be eleven-down on a crossword puzzle. She was sure that she would never be able to leave her bedroom again. She smoked two cigarettes, one after the other.

FIRE AND ASHES

Unaware of how mentally tired and drained she was becoming, the second cigarette slipped through her fingers and fell to the floor as she drifted into a fitful sleep. Jon's letter that she crumbled and attempted to throw in the waste can but missed was buried in the rug and was the cigarette's first victim. The paper quickly turned to ash and the sparks slowly began eating through her beautiful white fur rug. The sparks grew into a small flame as they started to burn the carpet beneath the rug. Diamond tossed and turned in a fitful sleep. Seduced by the smoke, she did not wake up. The fire, like a hungry animal, blazed a trail around the left side of her bedroom, first devouring her dressing table skirt and the hem of her imported satin drapes. Then it crept up the windows, scorching her ruffled Venetian shades, the ones she saved a month to buy.

Joe Jr. was emptying the garbage next door late that night because he had forgotten after dinner, and he didn't want his mother to see it in the kitchen tomorrow morning. He saw the smoke and flames coming from Diamond's windows. He dropped the garbage and ran into the house. His mother and father were on the couch dozing in front of the television. "Mama, mama! Ruby's house is on fire!"

Evelyn jumped off the couch and ran to the window. "Quick, boy, call the fire department. Tell them the whole side of the house is burning."

He ran to the kitchen telephone. "Operator, give me the fire department, quick." He was connected in what seemed like minutes, but were only seconds. I'm calling because a house is on fire. No, not my house, the house next door. 3206 Sutton Avenue. Four people, hurry please."

Evelyn shook her husband. "Joe, get up! The house is on fire!"

He wiped his eyes and ran around the room and into the kitchen and came back. Where's the fire?"

"Next door, Pearl's house. Junior, did you call the fire department?"

"Yes, ma'am."

"What did they say?"

"They're on the way."

I'm going upstairs to get some blankets. Joe, you and Junior go outside and see what you can do."

Pearl, the first one to smell the smoke, jumped out of bed and put on her robe. She ran to Ruby's bedroom. "Ruby, Ruby, wake up! There's smoke in the house! We have to get out!" Ruby was groggy and slow to respond, so Pearl pulled her out of the bed.

"Pearl, are you crazy? What are you doing?"

"Ruby, get up. We have to get out of here."

Ruby, wide awake now and smelling smoke, was frozen in fear. "Pearl, is the house on fire?"

"Yes, Ruby, let's go!"

"I have to get a coat, Pearl. I can't go in the street in baby doll pajamas." She quickly snatched a coat from the closet.

Topaz, in a nightgown, met them on the stairs with the same look of terror on her face. "Where is Diamond?"

Diamond awakened with a coughing fit from the smoke and realized the whole left side of her room was in flames. The dressing table and curtains were completely burned up, and the path to the windows was blocked by fire. She didn't panic. She knew she didn't have the luxury of fear, and she needed all her strength to get to the door.

She immediately rolled out of the bed and started crawling on the floor, trying to stay under the smoke to reach the door, the way she had taught her students year after year in fire drills, but she was too weak to crawl to the door.

In a shrill, hoarse voice, she began frantically calling for help. "Pearl, Topaz, Ruby! Open the door! I can't reach the knob! There's too much smoke! Help! Help! Help!"

Pearl and Topaz, frozen in fear, did not move. Ruby ran to the end of the hall to open her door, but the doorknob was so red hot it burned her hand. She shouted through the door.

"Diamond, I can't open the door! It's too hot!" She turned to Pearl. "What can we do?"

The fire truck sirens were screaming up Sutton Avenue. Topaz squeezed Pearl's hand. "Thank God you called the fire department."

Pearl was confused. "I didn't."

"It doesn't matter who called. We have to get out there and tell them we need help for Diamond." Topaz ran to the bedroom door. "Hang on, Diamond! The firemen are here! We're going out to get you help!"

They ran out of the house into the night, and Pearl stopped for a second to grab the family picture in the foyer that was her father's greatest treasure.

Once they got outside, Evelyn rushed to cover Topaz with a blanket she'd brought from the house. Topaz resisted at first. "I'm not cold."

Sensing her disorientation, Evelyn wrapped the blanket around her. "You can catch cold in the night air."

Joe Sr. asked, "Where's Diamond?

Topaz wailed, "She's still in the house! We couldn't get in her room!"

The fire department was parking and hooking up to the hydrant. Topaz bolted to the fire truck. "My sister is upstairs, trapped in her bedroom. Please, hurry and rescue her!"

"That's why we're here, miss." He quickly began to strap on his oxygen mask.

Joe Sr., watching from the sideline, knew seconds counted. To everyone's amazement, he ran into the burning house upstairs to Diamond's room and, with three kicks, broke the door down. Diamond was collapsed on the floor. He cradled her in his arms like a baby and carried her out of the house.

The fire contained to one room at that point rolled out into the hall, burning everything in its path. Flames jumped on the staircase, and Joe could feel the heat at his heels as he sprinted to the door.

Diamond weakly whispered in his ear. "Joe, you saved my life."

The fireman scolded Joe for risking his life. The Morgan sisters all kissed him with tears of thanksgiving for their sister's life.

Diamond inhaled so much smoke the fireman carried her to the fire department ambulance and placed her on the cot. "Miss, I'm just going to put this oxygen mask on your face to clear your lungs. We've already called the Red Cross, and a nurse will be here to check on you when they arrive. I have to get back to the fire." Diamond nodded her head and rested in their ambulance.

The house was in full blaze by this time. The firemen chopped down doors and windows, and the fire spilled onto the front and back lawns. Pearl, Topaz, and Ruby watched for over three hours as their childhood home burned to the ground. The gold and red flames were strangely beautiful and destructive at the same time, exploding from the house like fireworks.

Pearl never stopped clutching the family picture. "Topaz, can you believe that this is the only thing left? We didn't even save Mama's pearls."

Ruby was crying in Topaz's arms. "All my records and record player, my dancing trophies, everything, and all my stuff gone. We don't have any clothes, shoes, nothing."

Pearl looked to Topaz for answers. "How did this happen?"

"It doesn't matter how, Pearl. It just did. Instead of crying, I'm fighting hard to count our blessings. We're all safe. Thank God for the Cobbs. They were our guardian angels tonight. Everything material can be replaced. We came so close to losing Diamond. My heart breaks at that thought."

Pearl, head bent, was tearfully half talking to herself. "Our house is gone. Everything destroyed...it's like losing Mama and Daddy all over again."

Topaz stopped her before she could continue. "Pearl, stop. This isn't like it was then. This is horrible, but this time we're not lost. We have years of experience behind us, and now we can move past this."

Pearl lifted her head and wiped her eyes with her bath robe. "We do have fire insurance that we can split and start over."

"I'm not talking about money, Pearl. I'm talking about finally living the legacy of strength and faith that Mama and Daddy left us. Ruby, Mama used to always say, 'You have to have enough faith to believe that you will over-come, even when you can't see it, feel it, touch it, or taste it.'"

Pearl whispered, "Amen."

Topaz hugged Pearl. "It's time we stopped quoting it and started living it. This loss if forcing us to find our own way and stop depending on Mama and Daddy's house. We will be okay. You know Jones will help us. We can turn this around.

Ruby smiled. "Where is your church, Pastor Topaz?"

Diamond, resting on the cot in the ambulance, was glad to be alone with her thoughts. She inwardly thanked God for saving her life and saw it as an omen. Reading Jon's letter, she had wished for death. But now she was so grateful for life. She was sorry about the fire and the house, but she was sure it was a sign telling her it was finally time to start living the life she dreamed of for so long. Strangely she didn't feel guilty or sad; just relieved and excited about the future.

PEARL, DIAMOND, TOPAZ, AND RUBY

Jones Tabernacle, along with the Red Cross, did indeed help the sisters. Reverend and Sister Barnes invited them to live in the parsonage as long as they needed housing. The Red Cross donated fire emergency funds. Pearl, whose identity was the most shaken by the fire, was withdrawn for weeks until counseling with Reverend Barnes helped her find her center. He convinced her that she needed to work and feel productive.

With his encouragement, she began to send out applications for positions. She was very interested in an open position for a librarian. It was entry level, but she felt it was a job she could master. The only drawback was that it was in Grand Rapids. Reverend Barnes drove her down for the interview, and with his glowing recommendation of her organizational skills at the church, she was hired. Pearl was reluctant to leave Detroit, but she took a leap of faith and moved. She found an apartment and embraced and succeeded in her new life.

Diamond, the first to leave the parsonage, began searching for teaching positions in New York and Chicago. She never discussed the cause of the fire with her sisters and made a vow to herself she would take the secret to her grave. She got a call from Chicago to teach in a progressive public school three weeks before the semester started, and she accepted it over the telephone.

She was enchanted with the Windy City, the tall buildings, the L train, and the magnificent loop. She was so anxious to move she didn't have time to plan; therefore, she lived first at the YWCA, dressing every morning from her suitcase, until six months later, when she found an apartment.

She began dating her assistant principal her first year in Chicago, a widower with two teenage sons. She and Kenneth Johnson were married the first day of her second year in the city. The New Year's Day wedding was a beautiful celebration. Surrounded by Kenneth's sons and her three sisters, the bride was glowing in a rose petal peach velvet gown of her own creation. Diamond turned their home into a showplace, and every anniversary of their wedding they hosted a party that was the talk of the town for weeks.

Topaz helped Diamond pack and kissed her goodbye in the train station. She supported Pearl's decision to move. She rode with her and Reverend Barnes to the interview and took her to lunch to celebrate her first job. She missed the companionship of her sisters, and the adjustment to being without them on a daily basis was not easy for her. She made a ritual of calling them both each every Sunday evening.

Since the fire she had started to question her job at Good Shepherd. Being supervisor of nurses consisted of paper work and assigning duties, a prestigious title, but not the reason she loved nursing. The Red Cross nurses that night were nurturing and compassionate, the kind of nursing she realized she for longed for again. She missed the one-to-one human care that her office job did not provide. After much prayer and deliberation, she resigned at Good Shepherd and approached the Red Cross for a job.

The path was not easy. She was seen as overqualified for the job, and they didn't want to hire her for fear that, with her credentials, she would find the job not challenging enough. After four attempts she proved she was serious, and she landed the job. As Topaz was being fitted for her new uniform, she couldn't help but think how strange it was that something as awful as a fire could bring her a job where she felt fulfilled and needed.

Ruby was ashamed to admit to herself and anybody else how glad she was the fire forced them to move out of the house that had become a prison with three wardens. Moving into the crowded parsonage was still suffocating, so she sought refuge with the Kings. Pearl, too preoccupied with grief over their loss, did not stop her. Bishop and Sister King, overjoyed that she wanted to live with them, welcomed her with open arms.

She completed her senior year from their home. When she graduated from high school, the Kings gifted her with her own car. It was used, with a bad paint job, but it was a magic carpet to her and the ticket to the independence she craved. She immediately began auditioning for dance companies and was accepted by the Raymond Miller Troupe housed in the Fox Theatre in the downtown area. She was overjoyed.

Three years later she married Raymond Miller in the King's living room. Bishop King, now alone since Sister King's death a year earlier, proudly gave her away. Topaz was her matron of honor, and Pearl and Diamond stood by her side.

Two years later Bishop King passed away and willed his house to Raymond and Ruby. They turned the basement into a dance studio, and she and Raymond were able to teach dance from their home. Shortly after Bishop King's passing, Reverend Barnes blessed their first child at the altar of Jones Tabernacle. He was christened Shelton Curtis Miller.

Barbara Lewis is available for book signings
upon request. She can be reached via e-mail.
blewis1298@hotmail.com

BL1928@hotmail.con

b)